SURVIVING THE SINS

GLUTTONY

By

C. A. King

Cover Design:
SelfPubBookCovers.com/Ravenborn
Ravenborn Covers

Editor: J.D. Cunegan

Look for other books by C.A. King, including:

The Portal Prophecies:
Book I - A Keeper's Destiny
Book II - A Halloween's Curse
Book III - Frost Bitten
Book IV - Sleeping Sands
Book V - Deadly Perceptions
Book VI - Finding Balance

Tomoiya's Story:
Book I: Escape to Darkness
Book II: Collecting Tears

Surviving the Sins:
Book I: Answering the Call
Book II: Pride
Book III: Lust

When Leaves Fall: A Different Point of View Story

Peach Coloured Daisies: A Cursed by the Gods Story

Flower Shields: A Four Horsemen Novel

Miracles Not Included

Twisted Tales of A Dead End Street

Shot Through The Heart: A Faerie Tale

Cover Design: SelfPubBookCovers.com/Ravenborn
Ravenborn Covers

First Printing: November 16, 2018

ISBN: 978-1-988301-57-0

Kings Toe Publishing
kingstoepublishing@gmail.com
Burlington, Ontario. Canada

Prologue

Balance - the simple mention of the word has been known to invoke an image of a person walking on a tightrope, high above the ground, with no net. Each footstep would have to be placed carefully - outstretched arms teetering up and down, back and forth. Falling was never an option. In a performance, the rope was a short distance - in life, it never ended. It was that balance that made existence possible. To fail and tumble on either side could have been devastating. One trembling footstep steadied was the reason the next began to wobble. Cause and effect was a concept that should have been considered carefully by everyone. Unfortunately, it rarely was.

The Portal Prophecies may have saved the realms from Cornelius and Cornost, but by doing so, they opened doors to new problems at the same time. One could have said the metaphoric rope was shaken - its threads quivering. As a result, traversing it without tumbling became harder than it ever was before.

Change was inevitable in the universe. A plant that sprouted from the ground as a tiny shoot grew into a blooming flower and then withered away to seed. That very action brought new sprouts to life in the future. Some grew in the same spot, while others were whisked away by the wind to bring new scenery to lands previously untouched by their kind.

So, too, William's camp changed. The guardians were free to choose their own paths. Some returned to their homeland to help rebuild and others remained to establish new futures - choosing different keepers or to have none. The recently-formed symbiotic relationships between two life forces weren't created without their share of problems. Something was lacking - perhaps the synergy or trust that had been taken for granted in the past.

The camp itself split in several different directions. One group headed home with the guardians to rebuild their world for future generations. Those who remained in the camp swore oaths to continue to defend the portals. The Shinning brothers, Jessie, Dezi, and Pete, set out on a quest of their own to find a way to save their sister, Victoria, from the premature ageing that saving the lives of her family and friends caused her. Jade and Malarchy continued to forge a life in the political scene of the magical cities of the main world.

The forces that be searched for a new hero - one was chosen.

An ancient God, Mornyx, sent out minions born of emotions to use certain individuals as puppets. Their purpose was not only to aid in Morynx's escape, but serve up the chosen mate on a silver platter - a child destined to be born from the union.

Jade was determined that neither herself nor anyone else would turn out to be the Chosen One. Together with a growing group of misfit friends and a less-than-lucky leprechaun, she swore to stop Morynx's plans. With Pride and Lust already having achieved success, she had only five more chances to save herself and the world...

An Excerpt From Pride

Prudance stopped at the window to read the posted menu, hoping something would catch her eye. It did. She'd heard about magical shots before, but never tried one. The options looked promising.

There wasn't even a moment of hesitation. The outdoor patio, as nice as it was, wasn't a choice for her. The hot afternoon sun was pounding down on the pavement. Excess exposure could ruin the pale complexion she worked so hard to maintain - not to mention the wrinkles it could cause in later years.

She swung the door open. Every pore on her body relished the results of an overactive air conditioner. She could almost feel little beads of sweat freezing on the spot. For that reason alone, she was willing to overlook the appearance of the rest of the establishment.

It was by no means one of the five-star restaurants she had become accustomed to. By her standards, she was standing in a dive that wouldn't even score one star. Still, the place was cool; they had shots; and she was famished.

She waited impatiently for someone to seat her. Checking her watch every thirty seconds or so and tapping her feet wasn't making staff magically appear. After about ten minutes, she decided to find herself the cleanest table possible.

Glancing around, the room looked more like a bar than a cafe. The lights were dim and hung down over top of booths. She scoffed at the sight of bench seats that looked as if they had been removed from a church. A witch would have to be either very dumb or very drunk to be caught sitting in one of those. She, most certainly, wasn't either. She passed them by, opting for a more central location. A plain wooden table with two almost-matching chairs was the best option visible. She placed her purse on the ground under the table and waited.

She could understand it was off-peak hours and the afternoon rush would have been over, but someone should have been available to serve customers.

Prudance waited another five minutes. The pain sharpened. "Hello," she called out.

Her first attempt went unanswered.

"Hello!" she yelled a bit louder. "Is anyone here? I'd like to place an order."

"Just a minute," a high-pitched woman's voice yelled back.

Somehow, it sounded familiar, but Prudance couldn't place it. She simply shrugged her shoulders. At least someone was there who could take an order. She pulled a single-page menu out from between two shakers. Her eyes glimpsed over the offerings. Outside the magic shots had caught her attention. She forgot to check out the food selection.

Fried this... fried that. Yuck.

"What can I get you?" the waitress asked, finally making an appearance.

Prudance didn't look up. "Do you have a salad?" she asked. It had taken years for her to transform her body into the temple it now was. All that hard work wasn't going to waste in one afternoon. Most of the items listed weren't anything she would ever consider putting anywhere near her mouth.

"Does it say we have salads?" the waitress snapped back.

"No."

"Then we don't have salads."

The snarky tone of the waitress' voice wasn't something to easily let go. "I would like a BLT, hold the bacon, the bread and the mayo and add a fresh lemon. Oh, and I see you have an avocado dip. I'd like one of those - hold the dip part."

"You want a whole avocado?" the waitress snickered.

"Yes," Prudance answered. "Sliced. You can put it all in one bowl."

"You're serious?"

"Quite," Prudance answered. "Seems you do serve salads after all. Can I also have an iced lemon drink with a shot of concentrated channeling enhancement? Thank you."

She watched the girl stroll off to the back room again. The voice was so familiar, still she couldn't place where from.

It was obvious the two had never met before. The waitress had an appearance one simply didn't forget, considering her skin had an odd tinge to it. It was a mystery. The hairs on the back of Prudance's neck standing up was proof enough whoever she was, the waitress had strong magics at her command.

Why work here?

Lost in thought, she hadn't heard the footsteps approaching the table. A glass plunked down in front of her, its contents spilling over the sides.

"Be careful!" she yelled. Glancing up, she froze, locked in the gaze of two of the most perfect eyes she had ever seen. She searched for words, but came up with only one and in no more than a whisper. "Joseph."

"What are you doing here, Prudance?" he asked, glancing at the door as if expecting company any minute.

"You're alive," Prudance responded. "Why didn't you tell me you survived? I thought you died."

"Who sent you?" Joseph asked.

"Sent me?" Prudance repeated. "No one sent me. I came home for a visit and was out shopping."

The prince chuckled. "You don't come to places like this," Joseph commented. "So spill it. Why are you here?"

"I was hungry!" Prudance yelled back. So many emotions flowed through her body: anger that he hadn't told her he was alive; anguish that he wasn't happy to see her; disgust that she had fallen for him in the first place.

She felt the pain again, this time tearing at her heart strings instead of her stomach. It was easy enough to make this meeting nothing more than a distraction. Her pride was already at stake elsewhere and she wasn't about to let him abuse it here. Her face hardened - no longer that breakable porcelain that was in danger of cracking.

"And you," she snarled. "How the mighty prince has fallen. Working as a barkeep in a dive isn't where I would have ever expected to find you. I'd like to say you look good, but I'd be lying. You really do look like a washed-up has-been. Who's the green goblin? Your new girl?" She washed down the words with half of the iced lemon drink.

"Your pride is going to be your downfall," Joseph barked back, walking away. "She's my sister."

There was no time for regret; still it was there. A gem fell from her fingers, clanging on the table. It spun for a second before slowing to a resting spot.

"Keep the change," Prudance barked, already at the exit. She heard Joseph mumble something under his breath, but wasn't about to give him the satisfaction of looking back.

Hot air hit her face. She swallowed back the saliva pooling in her mouth. That familiar sickly feeling returned. If she had any colour in her face, it would have drained on the spot. In the background, she heard glass breaking and a shriek. She didn't move.

"Prudance!" Kasper yelled.

"Sorry," she answered, staring at nothing.

"Are you okay?"

"Kasper," Prudance said. "What a pleasure to run into you."

"Indeed," Kasper replied. "Are you alright?"

"Yes," Prudance replied. "Why do you ask?"

"Mainly because you have been standing in the doorway to this cafe for fifteen minutes," Kasper explained. "Through most of which, I've been calling your name. Perhaps you should come in and sit down."

The thought of returning and facing Joseph wasn't one she relished. The thought of spending time with the Director of Secrecy, Kasper Deogole, was even less appealing. "I'll be fine," she stated. "I think I had a bit too much sun today."

"I'll call for a car to take you home," Kasper offered.

"No," Prudance said. "I have a few things I ordered earlier today to pick up around the corner. I can take a cab from there. Thank you for offering, though."

"My pleasure," Kasper said, bowing his head. "Say hello to your mother for me."

"I will," Prudance replied, smiling. She glanced back from the sidewalk to watch the man disappear into the cafe. As soon as the door swung closed, she used one hand to brace herself against the side of a building. She took in a few sharp breaths of air trying to dispel the sickly feeling that seemed to plague her. Managing to regain her composure, she headed to the natural poisons and venom shop. There were a few more things on her list that she couldn't do without.

Chapter One

Joseph watched her strut to the exit. She was the one part of his past that he wished his father's memory-altering potion had erased. Who would have thought his one vulnerability would end up being a woman? Yet she was. Deep inside, he longed for the days they spent with one another in secrecy, hiding their budding relationship from both of their families.

Seeing her now simply reinforced his beliefs; without a kingdom behind him, he wasn't good enough for her. Prudance took pride in her pedigree. A barkeep wasn't the type of man she'd relish being seen with. She simply wasn't the sort to take a step down in status for the sake of love or any reason.

Love. He chuckled to himself. Was that what this was? Was a man with his past capable of loving anything?

His fingers fondled a tiny vial in his pocket, pulling it into view. He held it up, letting the illuminated contents hold his gaze until a loud crash stole his attention.

"Ow!" his sister complained, rubbing her arm. She scurried off to find a broom and dustpan.

"Are you okay?" Joseph asked upon her return. He briefly glanced at a bandage wrapped around the area just above her wrist. "Did you cut yourself?"

The broken bits of a variety of dishes pushed against each other, struggling for room in the dust pan. Once they were all loaded, they clanged together one final time, falling into a garbage container beside the bar.

"I'm fine." Her gaze fell upon the vial, eyes widening. "Tell me, brother, is that what I think it is?!" she shrieked. If looks could kill, there would have been nothing left of him. Daggers shot from her gaze, each one meant to extract as much damage as possible.

"Yeah," Joseph answered, ignoring his sister and returning his attention to the small bottle. He'd all but forgotten it was still locked between his thumb and forefinger, waiting.

"You've had it this whole time?" Zoe complained. "And you didn't tell me? We've been working in this disgusting place and starving while you had all that power in the palm of your hand? I deserve better than that."

"I agree, my sister, but you know we couldn't have used it," Joseph argued. "We were being watched and scrutinized. I didn't want to get your hopes up for a quick fix to our current situation." He shook the bottle, pursing his lips together as it turned opalescent before his eyes. "I've been waiting for exactly the perfect moment."

"And when exactly is that going to happen? Today... tomorrow... next year... twenty years from now? I demand to be a part of the plans as well. I want a feast!" Her eyes glowed green. "I want every type of delicacy in existence, all for me." She cackled. "Bring in a bunch of hungry orphans to watch me eat my fill, and when I'm done, I'll refuse them the scraps." Her voice hissed.

"Don't be a glutton, sister," Joseph ordered. "It doesn't become you." He shoved the vial back into his pocket, turning his attention back to wiping down the bar.

"I think we should use it," Zoe complained. "Why are we waiting? Have you lost your nerve?"

Joseph darted a glare in her direction. "We will... when the time is right and not a moment before." He sighed.

Letting his sister know about the potion was a misstep on his part. Virtuous, she was not. That included her lack of patience. Spontaneity had served her well in the past, but this was too delicate an opportunity to rush into. This was their last hope. If it failed, they could end up waiting tables for the rest of their lives.

A bell sounded, indicating a new customer had entered. Joseph glanced up, a sly grin forming as he eyed their new patron.

"I'd like a lemonade with a shot of charisma," Kasper yelled. "Make it snappy." He took a seat on the far side of the establishment at the least conspicuous table.

"Looks like opportunity just knocked," Joseph said, chuckling. "I think we should answer. Don't you, sister? I am positive a single shot of charisma isn't going to help that sorry sap of a man. Why don't you pull the blinds and lock the door so we can give him something a bit stronger?" He poured the contents of the vial into a tall glass before filling it to the brim with lemonade.

Zoe's smile matched her brothers. "An excellent plan," she cooed. "I'd say our future looks bright." She pulled out a pair of sunglasses, her last reminder of her life before her homeland was destroyed. Finishing her task, she turned in time to see an ice cold drink placed on the table directly in front of their soon-to-be victim. Having control of the Director of Secrecy was only the start to her plans - plans she had no intention of sharing, not even with her brother.

Chapter Two

The table wobbled, one leg being slightly shorter than the others. The weight of the drink had been enough to shift the balance. Kasper snatched up the glass, sending the surface back in the opposite direction in a noticeably uneven tilt.

The director gulped back the contents. "Ah. Another!" He held up the cup of ice, anticipating a refill. Pulling a handkerchief from his pocket, he dabbed the moisture forming on his brow. Two fingers loosened his collar. "Is the air conditioning broken?"

"No, sir," Joseph replied. "It might be the shot taking effect. Charisma is a strong request."

"Right," Kasper huffed, the words slurred. His head fell backwards, lips parted and nostrils flaring.

Joseph snapped his fingers in front of the director's face, watching for any movement. There was none, not even a blink. The potion had a hold of him tightly; a grip that was about to squeeze the man for every drop of lemonade the royal duo had been forced to serve since the downfall of their homeworld. If nothing else came of this, he planned to ensure they at least ended up with their wands returned.

"Kasper," Joseph said, waiting to see if there was an answer. Confident the director was under the influence of the potion, he continued. "I want you to forget we were ever enemies. As far as you are concerned, we have been on the same side since before we first met. You have been planning to offer my sister and myself cushy jobs with a substantial pay. Our advice in your ear is gold to you. You'll hang on every word we say and act on every suggestion. We are to be equally as important as you are. If anyone asks why the change of heart, you'll tell them we are aiding the department with a top secret initiative." He winked at his sister, watching before joining her a few feet away.

"Do you think that's good enough?" she questioned. "I want to be treated as a queen, not an employee. I don't care how much he pays me."

"Baby steps, sister," Joseph cautioned. "We will get there, but we can't afford to draw attention to our endeavours. There are those in power who still remember the happenings of the past. Kasper is but one man. I'm going to wash up in the back and change. I think I still have one decent suit left that will do for the occasion. Tonight, after we are done with Kasper, we celebrate our own victory."

Joseph glanced over his shoulder from the door to the back. His fingers fondled a second vial stashed safely in his pocket. As much as he loved and believed in his sister, that secret was one he wasn't about to let slip.

*****

Zoe chuckled, her eyes fixated on the director. She circled the table for two. As soon as her brother was out of sight, she pounced on her prey without hesitation.

"Kasper Deogole," she purred, licking her lips. "You will remember me as your only true love. You'd do anything for me and you'd listen to me over anyone else... including my brother. When you wake up, I want you to spend eternity providing me with everything I want, even if it means taking it from those who need or deserve it more. You'll do anything to secure my happiness. Oh... and you won't mention how you feel to anyone, including my family. I know you'll agree, relationships aren't meant to be in the limelight."

She backed away from the table, cackling. This was better than even she had imagined. A voice in her head painted pictures of treason against her own blood. The argument supporting her brothers and sisters coming first was compelling, but a stronger, silent one shot it down with force. The battle left a twinge of pain in her side, but a smile on her face.

"I suppose I should order something," Kasper said, coming out of his trance. He turned to face his waitress, his eyes widening at her sight.

"I was hoping you'd take me for lunch somewhere more expensive," Zoe stated.

"I was just thinking the same thing, my dear," Kasper replied. "I came to take you two out to discuss our future arrangements."

"My brother won't be joining us, I'm afraid," Zoe stated. "It'll be just the two of us." Her fingers glided over the man's shoulder. "That's okay, isn't it?"

"Of course," Kasper agreed. "Why don't you pick the location?"

"I'd be glad to," Zoe cackled. "I suppose I should change." She glanced at her clothes. "Something a little less conspicuous would benefit us both, I would imagine. Of course... you have my wand. Perhaps you could fetch it for me?"

"I'd be happy to," Kasper replied. "We can grab it on the way. It won't take but a minute."

"Excellent." Zoe unlocked the door, then waited for her date to open it before exiting. She glanced back for only a split second, watching the door close on part of her life. The pain in her side strengthened, subsiding only after she faced forward, embracing her new future.

"Zoe," Joseph called out, still straightening his tie. His hands fell to his sides at the sight of the empty room. He scratched his head. *Where did they go?*

Chapter Three

Esmerelda stopped outside the tavern, glancing at her own reflection in the window. The blinds being closed provided the perfect chance for a once-over before heading inside. Her lips rubbed together, evenly coating every crack with a homemade balm. A pat on the sides of her beehive do and she was ready for lunch with Kasper.

Ignoring the *Sorry, We're Closed* sign, she barged in, a nervous smile forming in the anticipation of an afternoon of romance. These once-a-week lunch dates were enough to keep her going until there was time to frolic on the weekend. Her smile intensified at the thought.

Esmerelda stepped inside with a spring to her step. Her jovial demeanour abandoned her at the door. The room was empty save for a single gentleman she didn't recognize.

"Can I help you?" Joseph asked, knocking over a toothpick tower he'd been building. He glanced up at the woman then back at the mess he'd just made, a scowl forming on his face from indecision. Did he clean it up, or leave it?

"I'm meeting the Director of Secrecy for lunch," Esmerelda stated. "I guess he's running a bit late. Do you know which table he usually sits at?"

Joseph chuckled. "He doesn't usually come here at all," he replied. "But he was here earlier. He left." One hand swooshed the toothpicks to the floor.

"He left?!" she exclaimed. "Did he leave a note or say where?" She took a seat beside him.

"Nope," Joseph answered. "I have no clue where good ole Kasper slunk off to."

"I'm sure something important came up," Esmerelda muttered.

"I doubt that," Joseph said, chuckling. "He took my sister with him. If I know her, he's giving her the best of everything. She wouldn't settle for anything less."

"Oh."

It was one simple word, but it held the emotions of a well-crafted sonnet written by a jilted lover. Joseph glanced over at the woman, instantly regretting the choice. Even her hair drooped, every curl weighted down under the burden of sadness. Their eyes met. The power of the gaze slapped him leaving a twinge of pain. He recognized the look. It was the same one Prudance had given him earlier. He thought she loathed his existence, but he had been mistaken. The woman sitting beside him made it all clear. How could he have been so wrong?

"Can I offer you a drink?" he asked. "It's on the house. We have a fix-all special today."

"Thank you," Esmerelda answered, her voice no more than a whisper.

He rounded the bar. After filling two glasses with ice and soda, he added the most expensive shot in the joint to both - the one that cured a heartache.

"I think I'll join you," he said, a huff escaping his lips. "I've been jilted twice today already. I think that deserves a little pick-me-up."

Chapter Four

Jade leaned back in her chair, reading the material Sarah printed out for her on the topic of the seven deadly sins. If there was any hope of stopping one, she needed to fully understand what they were. Figuring out the signs that came part and parcel with each was crucial. The only thing they knew precisely was each left a strange picture on its victim's skin; a branding of sorts. The things they didn't know formed a much larger list and included where to start their search.

"I'll trade a sweet tea for your thoughts," Malarchy offered, setting a cup on the desk in front of his daughter.

"That's a terrible deal," Jade scoffed and glanced at the drink without touching it. Drinking it meant accepting a reward. She'd done nothing to warrant such a gift. "My thoughts aren't worth it. I'm so frustrated with this whole mess. I don't even know if I'm coming or going."

Malarchy took a seat across from his daughter. "I wish I had the answers," he said, pinching the bridge of his nose. "But I don't. You look tired. Have you slept at all?"

"A little," Jade admitted, "probably not enough. It'll get better soon. The dreams are a bit easier to accept now that I know what to expect and it's always the same. It's the ending that worries me. If all seven puppets finish their work, what happens?"

Malarchy shook his head. "I think it's time we enlisted some other help. This is too big for our little circle." He leaned back in a chair, braced for an argument.

"What other help?" Jade questioned, a scowl showing its early beginnings on her face.

"Aye," Toby blurted out, appearing on the desk. "What other help ye be talking about? I like to think we have things under control at the moment. There have been no signs of the other sins."

"I disagree. The fact Jade is still having dreams is an indication the others will show up somewhere. We need help. I'm going to speak with Kasper," Malarchy said. He steadied his form, fully prepared for a backlash from his audience of two.

"You want to bring Kasper in because of me?" Jade shrieked. "I think we can handle it."

"I agree with the lass," Toby said, folding his arms over his chest.

"This has nothing to do with you, Jade!" Malarchy bellowed. "Yes, you are my daughter. And yes, I want you to be safe."

"So how does that have nothing to do with me?" Jade argued, her eyes stinging. The papers in her hand flew across the desk, knocking Toby backwards.

"I'm okay," the leprechaun mumbled, jumping back to his feet. His comment went unheard.

"Because there are other people involved too!" Malarchy yelled, standing. He rapped his white knuckles on the desk, sending vibrations across the surface.

"Whoa," Toby complained, wobbling again. "Perhaps I'll take a seat for the duration of this conversation." He fell backwards, landing on his bottom.

"There is more at stake here than just you!" Malarchy explained in a stern voice. "I was elected into office and I'm expected to see to the needs and safety of the magical community. Whatever is in that cave, I believe it is a threat. I don't see how we can leave it unprotected."

"Gavin is there, remember?" Jade muttered, her voice squeaking.

"Gavin isn't answering me anymore," Malarchy replied, his lips pursing together. "I think we need to face the facts; Gavin has jumped ship. None of us can rely on him from now on. That's not a statement, it's an order." He hung his head. "Bringing in Kasper isn't on the table for discussion. I'm sorry, Jade... I have to do it."

"Ye have ta do what ye have ta do," Toby agreed, a wicked grin crossing his face. "Of course, the lady could use one of her wishes."

"No wishes!" Malarchy ordered. "We don't need a bigger mess on our hands than we already have. You keep your magic and everything else in your pants."

"I take exception to that," Toby said, a feisty grin issuing a challenging. "There's nothing wrong with me magic or what's in me pants."

Malarchy snorted, ignoring the not-so-lucky leprechaun dancing some form of a jig on his daughter's desk. "It's for the best." He glanced back on his way out in time to see the unopened sweet tea landing in the garbage. He sighed, closing the door behind him. Perhaps one day she'd understand. A heartache was the better choice especially when the only other option was death.

If Morynx was in fact a vamprite god, a war was almost inevitable. Gavin was sure to take the side of his people. He couldn't rely on a vamprite to have Jade or anyone else's best interests in mind, at least not in this instance. Of course, he also hadn't given up on there being an amicable solution just yet.

Chapter Five

"Have a seat," Kasper offered, pointing to one of the two chairs across the desk from his own.

"This is your office?" Zoe asked, one lip raised in disgust. "I thought it would be bigger." She shrugged her shoulders, ignoring the offer of a chair.

"Yes, well," Kasper replied, "waste not, want not. That's my motto." He pointed to a plaque engraved with those words. "Riches don't grow on trees."

"Perhaps not for some," Zoe said, smiling. "I'll need my own office, if I am going to work here."

"Of course," Kasper agreed.

"It will have to be much bigger than this," Zoe continued. "I need space to work efficiently."

Kasper tapped two fingers on his temple. "I suppose it can't be helped. A happy employee is a productive one. I'll see to it."

"Get me a secretary too," she demanded, pushing a few books to the floor from their place on a shelving unit.

"What in the realms for?" Kasper complained. "I'm not exactly sure what it is I am going to be having you do, yet."

A pout formed over Zoe's lips. "I have always wanted my own secretary. You won't deny me that bit of happiness, now will you?"

Kasper's fingers tapped a little harder, leaving a red spot. "Of course not," he replied. He pressed a black button on his desk. "Petra, would you come here please?"

"Is that an intercom?" Zoe gasped. "I want one of those too." She rushed over to the device. A long red fingernail pressed down on the button. "Is anybody out there?"

Kasper swatted her hand away, his eye twitching. "It's not a toy. I'm the only one in the department that has one," he explained. "How would it look if I gave one to the new employee as well?"

"But it's so perfect, Kaspi," Zoe said, her pout increasing exponentially. "We could be the only couple to have matching intercoms in Pewterclaw. Speaking of looks, you haven't said a word about what you think of my new appearance."

Zoe twirled around, allowing frills to swirl - her signature black ensemble having been traded in for a more feminine red dress. That wasn't the only thing that changed. The light green tinge to her skin was also hidden in illusion. Only those who knew her well would be able to figure out her true identity.

"You would look lovely in anything, my dear," Kasper offered without glancing up from his desk.

"It does feel good to have my wand again," Zoe said, a fire dancing in her brilliant green eyes. With a swoosh, a compact and bright red lipstick appeared out of thin air. The mirror clicked open. After applying a thick layer of ruby gloss to her perfectly plump lips, she puckered them. "Muah!" Her rump planted on a corner of Kasper's desk, legs apart in the most unladylike position.

"You wanted to see me, sir," Petra said from the door. "Is everything alright?" She glanced from Zoe to her employer, then back again.

"Fine," Kasper replied. "Everything is fine. This is Zoe. She's going to be doing some sensitive work within the department and I'll need you to assist her. You can start by finding her a rather large office."

"The largest office," Zoe barked.

"Yes... as I was saying," Kasper continued, "the largest office in the building will do and see to anything else she needs while you are at it."

"Sir," Petra stuttered. "The biggest office belongs to the commander in chief. I don't think he'll be happy giving up the space. He is already quite cramped with all the paperwork he does."

"I don't think the director is paying you to think!" Zoe snapped. "Know your place and follow his orders. I'd like to see my new office now."

"Sir?" Petra froze, waiting for the director to say something... anything.

"Whatever Zoe wants," Kasper muttered, making a shooing motion with his hand. "I have work to do. Please handle it, Petra. I'd appreciate as few interruptions as possible. I feel a horrible headache coming on. Thank you, ladies... off you go."

"I'd like my office moved to be across from Kasper's," Zoe ordered. "You are writing this down, aren't you? I don't want any mistakes."

Petra flipped open a steno pad. "Of course," she squeaked. "Office across from the director's... got it. Anything else?"

"I'll need a clothing expense account," Zoe said. "Actually, a general expense account."

"I'm not sure we have those," Petra replied.

"We do now," Zoe stated, waggling her eyebrows. "Where is the office? I'll need to check it out to see how much redecorating it needs."

Petra's forehead wrinkled. "Redecorating?" she echoed. "The director doesn't have any funds allocated for that. The budget is already set. He is a very efficient man. I don't think there is a penny left to squeeze."

"Then reallocate," Zoe demanded. "You did hear Kasper say I was to have anything I wanted, didn't you?"

"Here we are," Petra said, pointing to a frosted glass door. "We probably shouldn't disturb the commander until he's been filled in on the situation."

Zoe sighed. "Out of the way," she barked, opening the door and walking in. "What a mess!"

The room was a basic grey colour, with overfilled filing cabinets lining every wall from top to bottom. Papers lay scattered about in what their owner called *a controlled mess.*

The commander sat at his desk, the look of confusion on his face growing as each second ticked by. "To what do I owe the honour?" he asked. Only a select few of the highest-ranking military personnel or Kasper himself had authorization to visit his office.

"I'll need all of this gone!" Zoe ordered, shaking her head. "The room should be painted... something green would be nice. Do we have any catalogs for furniture?"

"What in the blazes is going on, Petra?" the commander yelled. "I am trying to work. This interruption is an outrage. I'll never finish these reports on time."

"I'm sorry, sir," Petra answered. "It's just..."

"This isn't your office anymore," Zoe blurted out. "Kasper is moving you. I'll be taking over this one. You'll need to pack and rather quickly."

"It's about bloody time I got more space," the commander said. "I've been bothering that man for ages. Where am I moving to?"

"Yes..." Petra stuttered. "About that... I'm not exactly sure, yet. This is a reorganization in progress."

"I see," the commander replied, rubbing his well-trimmed beard. "How am I to give up this space if I don't have anywhere to move to?"

"Like I said," Petra continued, "it's a work in progress. I have quite a bit of reshuffling to do."

"Is this your family?" Zoe questioned, picking up a picture. An ache surged through her midsection at the thought of her own. She replaced the photograph, biting her lip. The word family itself caused her pain.

"Yes..."

"I need my office," Zoe complained, her foot tapping. "Is that a storage room? I can use that." She pulled open a door to find a room filled to the brim with more files.

"Those are sensitive subjects!" the commander exclaimed, a scowl plastering over his previously content appearance. "You are not cleared to even breathe in the same room as them. I must insist..."

"Actually," Zoe hissed, "I have full clearance around here... Kasper's orders." She cackled. "Oh, don't have a meltdown. I have no interest in your paperwork and no plans to read any of it."

"What exactly is it you will be doing?" the commander asked, leaning back in his well-worn chair.

"That's classified," Zoe whispered. She held a finger up over a devious smile. "Sh..."

The commander's face reddened, his teeth grinding. A pencil snapped in his grip.

Petra offered a nervous chuckle. "Perhaps Zoe, you could pick out the décor while I make the rest of the arrangements. It'll be a few hours before a team can set up everything you need. In the meantime, there is a staff birthday party going on in the main lobby. Perhaps you'd care to join in and meet the rest of the team?"

"A party," Zoe cooed. "Is there cake?"

"Yes, I believe so," her new aide answered.

"Then I will attend," Zoe agreed. "I expect you will have everything handled swiftly..."

"Of course," Petra replied. "Let's head down and I'll introduce you before finding the selections available for your new office."

"Fine," Zoe said. "Commander, I suggest you start packing. I'd like to have this transaction over and done with before the end of the day."

The commander glared in her direction, eyes bulging from their sockets. Another minute and he might have exploded.

Petra ushered Zoe out the doorway. Kasper would have to deal with any staff put off by the new arrangements. As a mere secretary, she wasn't paid enough to clean up any extensive messes.

Chapter Six

The gathering in the lobby was finishing a rendition of a well-known birthday song when the two women arrived. Paper confetti and streamers floated through the air, disappearing on contact as they hit the floor.

"If I could have your attention. I'd like to introduce our newest team member, Zoe!" Petra announced. "Kasper hired her himself. I know you'll all offer her a warm welcome!"

"Thank you," Zoe purred, her arms pushing her secretary backwards away from the spotlight. "I'm honoured to be here. I can't believe you went to all this trouble!"

The rest of the staff exchanged glances. "We didn't do anything," a young woman sitting at the front table explained, shaking her head.

"No need to be modest," Zoe purred. "This is beyond even my expectations. You even got me a cake!"

"It's Howard's birthday..." the woman stated.

"What a coincidence," Zoe said, her smile straining not to falter. "You really should throw him a party sometime, too." She wandered over to the table, plunging her hand in the middle of the cake. Her tongue protruded, licking the icing from each finger. "This is good."

Gasps went unanswered.

Zoe took another handful, destroying every possible piece that could have been cut and leaving behind only a pile of mush. "Delicious," she said, an unnerving smile crossing her lips. "It was exactly what I needed. Petra, where are those catalogs?"

Petra forced a momentary smile. "Right over here," she replied. "You can look through them in my office while I rearrange things."

Chapter Seven

The door shook as it squeaked open. "Sir," Petra mumbled, sticking her head inside the office.

"What is it now?" Kasper asked, still rubbing his temples raw.

"I wanted to speak to you about the new employee," Petra admitted. "She is asking for some rather elaborate things."

"And?" Kasper questioned.

"I need to know," Petra stuttered, "where am I taking the money from to pay for them? There isn't anything in the budget for new office décor."

"Take some out of the unnecessary programs," Kasper ordered.

"Which programs are those?" Petra asked.

Kasper sighed, forcing his full attention to the woman pestering him. "Office parties, bonuses... cut back on supplies, if you have to. I don't care. Just find what you need."

"I don't think you understand the extent of the requests the young lady is making," Petra blurted out. "She wants three of the most expensive office chairs, in case she feels more productive in a different one from time to time. There are senior staff who have been on a waiting list for years for a new chair, myself included. How do I justify that to them?"

"You don't," Kasper argued. "If anyone wants to complain, show them the door... yourself included. I don't expect my tactics to be questioned. Have I done something to cause the staff here to doubt my abilities?"

"No, sir," Petra replied, her gaze focused down.

"Good," Kasper stated, smiling. "Then I guess there are no other issues for me to deal with."

"None, sir," Petra muttered, turning her attention to a knock on the door.

"Come," Kasper bellowed. "Ah, Joseph. Good to see you. What brings you to my office? Wait, I know. You are here to see your beautiful sister."

Joseph side-eyed the woman, obviously wanting a clear path from the room. He stepped to one side to accommodate her needs, offering his standard charming smile.

Petra flushed red, fanning herself with the steno notebook containing Zoe's instructions. "Thank you," she said, a sigh escaping off her lips at the end of the words.

"Petra," Kasper said, "please let Zoe know her brother is here."

"Of course," Petra gushed, adding a giggle. She stood in the doorway staring.

"Today would be good, Petra," Kasper ordered. "We don't want to keep the young man waiting."

"Of course," Petra replied again. She glanced back twice before fully shutting the door.

"I was actually here to see you," Joseph admitted. "We do still have a discussion about a job outstanding."

"Yes... so we do," Kasper replied, a lopsided grin spanning his face.

"Joseph!" Zoe exclaimed, entering the room. "I was wondering how long it was going to take you to come around. Don't get up, Kasper. I'll show my brother everything he needs to see." Linking arms with her brother, she led him across the hallway.

A team of decorators scurried about, placing furniture and arranging everything exactly as she requested.

"Leave us... for now!" Zoe ordered. "I have some pressing business to attend to."

"What's going on, sister?" Joseph asked. "Why did you disappear with Kasper?"

"You aren't jealous, are you?" Zoe asked, her signature devilish grin making an appearance. "I simply wanted to come ahead and make a few arrangements. I figured you'd find your way here sometime and catch up."

"And the new look?" Joseph questioned.

"It's hard to be green," Zoe said, pouting. "I wanted to fit in." Within a moment, her appearance switched to jovial. "I have my wand back." She waved it around, teasing him. "Don't frown, brother. It doesn't suit you. Your wand is in that room. I know you want it."

A grin formed over Joseph's face. "In there?" He hurried over to the storage closet and swung the door open.

The inside was less of a closet and more of a small sitting room, holding limited furniture; namely a couple of chairs and a display case. The latter contained his wand.

Excitement surged through his veins at the thought of filling one of the voids in his life - magic. Once that was satisfied he would work on the other. Prudance would be his again.

He lifted the glass enclosure, his mouth watering in anticipation of the power the small black stick held. One hand lunged forward, grasping it tightly.

"It's good to have this back," Joseph said, sighing. He turned to his sister, his breath labouring. "What have you done? What is this I am feeling?"

"You should take a seat, brother," Zoe ordered. Pushing him with two fingers, he fell backwards into a chair. "It's a little spell I came up with. I realized having power is great, but having more power is...

better." She cackled. "You are now my own personal little battery pack. Oh, don't try to speak. It'll only become harder for you. All you are meant to do from now on is sit there and lend me your everything."

Zoe glanced back at Joseph before closing the door on him. Her hands grasped her sides, feeling the familiar twinge of pain that accompanied any thoughts of her family. That, however, was easy enough to rectify... she simply wouldn't think about them anymore.

Chapter Eight

"Come!" Kasper yelled, frustration taking its toll on his demeanour. He glanced up, fully anticipating another bout of complaints about his new employee. "Malarchy. To what do I owe the honour of your presence?" His chair squeaked with resentment as he leaned back. "Business or pleasure?"

"Business," Malarchy replied. "But strictly off the books. I have a delicate matter to discuss with you."

"Sounds fascinating," Zoe purred from the door.

"This is my new associate, Zoe," Kasper announced. "She is helping me with a few... things."

"A pleasure," Malarchy said, bowing his head. "This is, as I said, a delicate matter..."

"Anything you can say to me, you can say to Zoe," Kasper declared. "She has full clearance."

"That's quite an accomplishment," Malarchy stated. "You must have done something extraordinary to have earned Kasper's undivided trust." He held out his hand.

Zoe laughed, ignoring his offer. "I'm afraid I don't trust quite as easily. Please pretend I'm not here. I'm sure whatever you have to say will be most fascinating, but of little relevance to me."

"Very well," Malarchy agreed. "It has come to my office's attention that the damage Atlantis did trying to rise in this realm was more extensive than we originally thought."

"How so?" Kasper asked, dropping his pen on the desk. It followed a slope to one side. The catalog currently being used to even the legs had been compressed enough to warrant being switched out for a newer one.

"A team of associates discovered a cavern sealed by magics from long ago. During one of the quakes we experienced, a crack formed in the walls. Some form of ancient seal was broken, threatening to release whatever it was meant to keep confined within," Malarchy explained, keeping his gaze on the director's strange new associate.

"And I suppose you know what is on the inside?" Kasper asked.

"It is reported to be an ancient god named Morynx," Malarchy answered.

"A god," Kasper repeated, chuckling. "If I believed in such deities, it might be of concern. Need I remind you that most of the magical people in this realm could be considered a god by the terunji?"

"Yes," Malarchy answered, arching his eyebrows. A crooked smile crossed his face. "But this one is reported to be the one from where the vamprite originated... a vampire god capable of turning the light of day into pure darkness."

"With all your squawking about vamprite rights, I'd have thought you'd relish the idea of finding their origins. Why are you coming to me?" Kasper asked, pursing his lips together. "You must know I'd have no interest in preserving anything remotely connected to their kind."

"I have no desire to let any one person, god or otherwise, rule all that is," Malarchy explained. "Vampire or not, I cannot allow this realm to be plunged into darkness for the sake of one race. I do have an oath to uphold."

"I'll buy that," Kasper admitted, nodding. "What of your daughter and her relationship?"

"This has been too taxing on them," Malarchy stated. "They are not currently on speaking terms. Although I should mention he is currently at the site, along with some of his associates."

"What else can you tell me about this Morynx?" Kasper questioned. "Something useful, I hope. You don't expect my office to do all the legwork."

Malarchy chuckled. "We have some information," he replied. "There is a dial that spins in the cavern through where the fissure runs. It has numerous symbols carved on it. With a movement similar to a clock, the hands change positions. When they do, simultaneously the opening grows as well. Once the gap is big enough, it is believed Morynx will escape."

"And steal the light of day?" Kasper asked.

"It isn't clear, exactly," Malarchy started, "but it is believed that Morynx's power is limited. The information we have gathered suggests a union of some sort is needed in order to conceive a child. Hand in hand, Morynx and that child shall rule all of darkness... the light having been extinguished."

"Well," Kasper said. "That is an interesting tale. I suppose you have a file for me?"

Malarchy smiled. "Of course," he said, tossing a folder from his briefcase on the desk. "Everything you need is in there. I trust you will afford me the luxury of updates."

"If we decide to do anything," Kasper answered, "I will keep you in the loop. I can't promise anything until I've sent a team to see what's what. You do understand?"

"I do," Malarchy replied. "It was a pleasure to meet you, Miss." He bowed in Zoe's direction.

"Likewise," she answered, forcing a smile as she watched him exit.

"Do you think he is telling the truth?" Zoe questioned. "Could there be a god hidden away in a magical cave?"

"I suppose anything is possible," Kasper answered. "Don't worry, though, we'll take care of it if there is."

His words faded, lost among her own thoughts. *A god who wants a child.* The woman who bore such an offspring would surely have more than she desired; more than she needed. She had a new purpose... to be made a goddess.

Chapter Nine

Esmerelda's normally high and poofy hair drooped, office supplies scattering all around her. She didn't have to meet any of her colleagues eye to eye to know they had taken over her favourite pastime. Normally, if there was any juicy information to be shared, she was the one to do it. Being the subject of gossip was as depressing as knowing everything being said was true.

Whispers of Kasper closing down the most expensive restaurant in the city for a mysterious woman sent her over the edge. She busted into Jade's office, blubbering incoherently.

"Slow down," Jade suggested, passing a tissue box across her desk. "I can't understand a word of what you are saying." Her face softened, offering the hope of consolation.

"I don't know what to do," Esmerelda cried. The blowing of her nose was accompanied by a loud honking noise. No amount of sniffling or otherwise was going to help her naturally nasal sounding voice, though. "How could he do this to me?"

"How could who do what?" Prudance asked from the door. "Did we miss something?" She glanced at Jessica and Krissy, then back to the distraught woman.

"Kasper," Esmerelda shrieked. Another round of sobs wet half the box of tissues before stopping. "He's seeing another woman." Her voice shook.

"Who is seeing another woman?" Simon asked.

"Kasper," all the women said in unison.

"Really?" Simon replied. "That's a bit odd, don't you think? I couldn't imagine another woman..." His voice faded, realizing the woman crying in front of him was clearly in love with the man.

"When did all this happen?" Jade asked. "Everything was fine a few weeks ago."

"It's been just about that long since I've seen him," Esmerelda admitted. "We planned to meet for lunch. There's a little place that Kasper claimed sold the best magical enhancement shots. He wanted me to try it..." Her voice faded into sobs.

"Downtown?" Prudance asked. "I ran into Kasper heading into that dive."

"It's not a dive!" Esmerelda argued. "Kasper would never take a lady to a dive."

Prudance nodded. "You're right," she lied, not wanting to upset the woman further. "But if I saw him heading in, presumably it was the same day you were to meet him."

Esmerelda nodded, tears streaking down her face. "He was there. The gentleman tending bar told me so."

"Gentleman," Prudance scoffed. "I'm not sure that word applies."

"Did he say why he left or where he went?" Jade questioned.

"The man said Kasper left with his sister," Esmerelda replied, heading straight into another bout of blubbering.

"The green goblin?!" Prudance blurted out.

"What did you say?" Simon asked. "What was her name?" He grabbed her by the arm, squeezing it for information.

"Ow!" Prudance exclaimed. "I don't know. Let me go..."

"Why did you call her that?" Simon asked, refusing to relinquish his hold.

"Because she had green skin," Prudance blurted out. She stumbled backwards, rubbing her arm. "I should turn you into a frog for that. Or, better yet, a wart on a frog." Her wand appeared in her hand.

"Enough!" Malarchy bellowed. "What are the lot of you doing?"

"She knows something about one of my sisters," Simon declared. "I've looked for signs of them everywhere."

"Your sister," Prudance echoed, her upper lip raising. "I only know about Joseph's sister."

"You know my brother, too?" Simon questioned, a rage building in his eyes.

"Brother," Prudance repeated. "Huh. The only brother Joseph ever mentioned was Lance. I wonder why that is?" A vicious grin formed at the end of her words.

"How is it you know him?" Simon took a step forward, but found himself blocked by Malarchy.

"We dated," Prudance announced.

Simon howled a laugh. "Joseph doesn't date. He is... rather fond of variety."

"Apparently, he didn't share everything with you," Prudance replied. "We were quite exclusive. I lost track of him after Lance destroyed your homeworld. I thought him to be dead until he served me my drink. Needless to say, I didn't stay long enough to catch up."

"What does this have to do with Kasper?" Esmerelda asked, sniffling.

"If he left with my sister," Simon said, "there has to be a reason." He pinched the bridge of his nose. "I can't see what that would be, though. Of course, everything relies on how accurate our information is..."

"What is that supposed to mean?" Prudance asked, her wand ready for a fight.

"Enough!" Jade yelled. "How can we hope to stop one of the sins from happening if we can't control those very emotions amongst ourselves?"

"She's right," Krissy said, coming out from hiding under the desk. "We need to stop arguing and work together. If magic starts flying in here, one or more of us are sure to be hurt. We can't afford for that to happen. We need all the help we can get to solve the bigger problem."

"Where does any of this leave us?" Jessica asked. "We know Kasper left with one of Simon's sisters but we don't know which one or to where."

"Actually," Malarchy admitted, "I think I do. I visited Kasper today. He had a young new associate who was using some form of illusion on herself. I almost missed the signs it was so subtle. He introduced her as Zoe."

"Zoe," Simon said, taking a seat. "How is she mixed up with the director? If anything she should want to stay miles away from the man." He shook his head.

A knock on the door interrupted their discussion. Jade glanced at her father for approval before inviting them in.

"I'm sorry to disturb," Petra said. "The front desk said I could find you here, sir."

"Please call me Malarchy. What can I do for you? You are a long way from the Department of Secrecy."

"Okay... Malarchy," Petra replied, her voice nothing more than a whisper. "I think there is something wrong with the director."

"Kasper?" Malarchy asked, his eyebrows arched. "Yes. I noticed he wasn't quite himself."

"His new employee," Petra continued, wringing a pair of gloves into knots in her hands, "is ordering things left and right. The director, as you know, is a frugal man and yet he is allowing her to have her way. She even had me collect all the pencils in the entire building for her use only. What could one person need with all those pencils?"

"Interesting," Malarchy muttered, rubbing is chin. "Do you know what it is he hired her to do?"

"No," Petra answered. "If you ask me, she's nothing more than a glutton."

"Gluttony," Jade muttered, her mind wandering to Jessica's notes still strewn about her desk. "You don't think Kasper could be..."

"Thank you, Petra," Malarchy said, interrupting his daughter before she revealed more than was necessary. He escorted the secretary to the door. "We'll look into it. I need you to do something for me... return to work as if nothing happened. Can you do that?"

Petra nodded. "I can. Thank you, sir... Malarchy." The door shut.

"If Kasper is under the spell," Simon said, "that isn't good news."

"No," Malarchy agreed. "It isn't. That will make the situation much harder to get a grasp on. He is a well-protected man."

"I'll be right back," Prudance announced, slipping out the door.

Her feet shuffled at double their normal rate. A sigh of relief escaped her lips as she caught up to Petra exiting the building.

"Thank goodness you aren't gone yet," Prudance said, putting her hand out to stop the motion of the door.

"Was there something else you needed from me?" Petra asked.

"Yes. I need to know if at any time you heard any mention of Zoe's brother." Prudance replied.

"Why yes," Petra answered. "That man is hard not to notice, being so handsome and all. He stopped by the other day. It was the oddest thing. He went into Zoe's office, but I never saw him leave and trust me, I was watching. I wanted to see if he is as perfect from the back as he is from the front. Does that mean something to you? He's not involved in what's happened to the director, is he?"

Prudance shook her head. "No I don't think so, but could you do me a favour?" she asked, pulling out a notebook from her purse and scribbled down a few words. "I need you to tell Zoe that a strange woman bumped into you at lunch and asked you to deliver this message. All she needs to do is respond in writing. It will find a way back to me with her answer."

Petra reached forward to take the paper. Her fingers gripped one edge, but Prudance hadn't yet released the other.

"Make sure," Prudance warned, "she believes this was a chance meeting."

"I will," Petra answered.

Prudance let go. "Thank you."

Chapter Ten

Prudance took stock of the glares shooting in her direction. "The hospital called," she lied, cool as a cucumber. "With all the noise in here, I never would have heard a thing."

"And?" Malarchy pried.

"And," Prudance answered, avoiding eye contact, "there is no change in my mother's condition. What did I miss?"

"We were discussing what to do about Kasper," Simon explained. "It makes sense that he would be a target with his proximity to Jade."

"The only way to find out for sure is to search him for the mark. According to these notes," Jade said, waving papers in the air, "it would be a picture of a pig. Any volunteers?"

"Not me," Simon blurted out, shaking away the image that formed in his mind. "Esmerelda, perhaps you might do the honours?"

"He's not even returning any of my messages," Esmerelda cried. "How do you expect me to undress him?"

Toby shivered. "I picked the wrong time to enter this conversation." He shook his head. "I'm gonna regret asking, but why are ye planning on having the director get naked?"

"To look for the mark, of course," Krissy replied, rolling her eyes.

"I think I'll be leaving this part in yer trusty hands," Toby announced. "I'll be back when I finish burning the image from me head." He disappeared in a puff of smoke.

"Useful little guy, isn't he?" Simon jested.

"Maybe we could catch the director alone," Jade suggested. "He must be heading home soon."

"That won't work," Esmerelda replied. "He doesn't disclose his home address to anyone. I've never been there. He prefers to visit me. It isn't even in the City's records. "

"Remind me to rectify that when this is all over. The city records part, that is. You'll have to take care of knowing his address on your own, Esmerelda. You may want to put some thought into your relationship." Malarchy suggested, slouching back in a chair.

"I've been thinking about that for a while now," Esmerelda admitted. "I guess I was worried he'd break it all off if I did."

"You need to have faith in yourself," Prudance replied. "No man should treat you poorly." Her eyes glossed over, realizing she needed to take her own advice.

"Maybe we could get back on topic? Let's deal with life-threatening before heartbreaking issues." Malarchy complained. He paused for any arguments. Satisfied there weren't any, he continued, "Right then. The best we can do is an early morning visit. Of course, with Zoe there that might be a problem."

"I'll handle my sister," Simon offered. "I know her better than anyone else."

"Are you sure?" Jessica inquired, concern dripping from her words. "This is the first time you've seen any of your siblings since..."

"No better time for a family reunion," Simon interrupted. "I can handle Zoe. Joseph, on the other hand, is another story. He'd have to have his guard down to be bested by anyone. That doesn't happen often, even with family. If he's involved, our chances of success are nil."

"I'll have Stan back you up," Malarchy offered. "He knows what's at stake. Our list of trustworthy alliances has grown slim as of late."

"What should we do?" Jade asked.

"Get some sleep," Malarchy suggested. "I have a feeling we will need it."

Chapter Eleven

"What's this?" Zoe snarled, examining the neatly folded paper. Her fingers traced the crisp edges as a subtle lavender fragrance floated up to tickle her nose.

"A message... a woman at lunch asked me to deliver it to you," Petra replied.

"What woman?"

"I don't know," Petra stuttered.

Honestly," Zoe huffed, "are we playing some teenage game of pass the note in class? I have no time for this."

"She told me to tell you to write your reply and it would find a way back to her," Petra blurted out. "Then she disappeared before I could say a word. I thought it might be important."

"It would find a way back," Zoe repeated, eyeing the paper now lying on her desk. Her eyes narrowed. "That's an interesting bit of magic... if it's true." A long red fingernail tapped on the desk, leaving indents in the wood. "Why would someone go through the trouble?"

"You could open it and see what it says," Petra suggested.

"I could, couldn't I?" Zoe shrieked. "Why in the realms didn't I think of that? I know... because it could be a trap. Did you think of that before making your snarky little suggestions? I think not. That is why I am on this side of the desk and you are... well, whatever you are." She pushed one chair away and pulled another behind her.

"I could send for the commander," Petra offered. "They have a team that sniffs out things like this."

"No." Zoe waved one hand in the air. "That man is still sulking over the loss of this office. He'd be of little use to me. I'll have to figure this out myself. Why don't you go make sure the team is ready for my expedition?"

"Of course," Petra replied, backing the room.

Zoe eyed the plain paper from both sides, jerking back with each movement, half expecting something to jump out at her. Nothing soon became a bore. Her finger teased at the edges, pulling back no more than a sliver at a time.

"Peek-a-boo," Zoe cackled, "I see you. Somebody has the audacity to call us out, brother." She glanced at the closet door. "I wonder who it is." Her attention returned to the fully opened note lying flat in front of her.

I know everything. It's time to meet. Choose the location and time. Come alone.

"Who indeed," she mumbled, heading across the hall. "Kasper."

"You could knock," he grunted.

"This is important," Zoe argued.

"And the intercom I had put in for you was for what?" Kasper questioned. "As much as I adore you, I do still have a job to do."

"This is about the job," Zoe stated.

"Really?" Kasper replied. "What do you need? Petra has seen to everything you wanted. Tereza sent over her finest expert on ancient symbols and markings... Majesta I believe her name is."

"I need to know who the most powerful witch in Pewterclaw is," Zoe blurted out.

"Most powerful witch," Kasper repeated, pursing his lips together as he reclined in his chair. "Up until a little while ago, that would have been Delilah. Of course she's in a coma at the moment. It's rather odd I just finished reading Malarchy's report on it this morning. I suppose her daughter, Prudance, would be the next in line."

"The report is part of what's going on in that cave, isn't it?" Zoe pried.

"Yes," Kasper replied.

"I should look at that," Zoe stated. "There might be some clues as to what we are up against."

"That's probably a good plan," Kasper agreed. He tossed a file folder on the corner of his desk. "Return it once you are done."

"I will," Zoe replied, already entering her own office. "Prudance." She opened the file to a familiar picture. "Salad girl. Had some trouble with the family... how interesting... I suppose it is time we find out where you fit into the picture so I can erase you from it."

With a reply scribbled on the back, the note folded itself back up, scrunching into a ball, before reopening into a beautiful lilac-coloured butterfly. Delicate wings fluttered open and closed; a magical paper-airplane ready for takeoff. Once airborne, it floated majestically towards the only window.

Zoe cackled, watching it. "It doesn't open," she sang. "Bad luck..."

Her words faded, self-righteousness morphing into anger. Her eyes burned red, hatred spilling over as hot as lava from an active volcano.

The butterfly was gone, having passed through the glass. All that was left in its place was a fleeting memory and a trail of purple glitter.

Her mood shifted once again. "Have your little victory, Prudance. Tonight we'll see who walks away laughing."

Chapter Twelve

The light flicked on. "Where do you think you are going?" Jade asked.

"I couldn't sleep," Prudance lied. "I thought I'd go for a walk to relieve some tension."

"Okay," Jade said. "I'm going with you."

"No, you're not," Prudance argued. "I'd like to be alone. You should get some rest."

"I'm the one with nightmares, remember?" Jade replied. "I don't want to sleep. I'm going with you." She untied her housecoat, revealing she was fully dressed, shoes and all. "If you want, I can follow behind."

"This could be dangerous," Prudance explained. "I don't want you getting hurt."

"If it is dangerous, that's all the more reason for me to go along." Jade held the door open, motioning with one hand for her friend to exit first. "There's safety in numbers."

"Two isn't exactly numbers," Prudance argued.

"Three," Toby said, appearing on Jade's shoulder. "I be watching out for my ladies."

Prudance rolled her eyes. "As long as Jade wants to use a wish," she mumbled.

"It's still help," Toby complained.

"Alright," Prudance conceded, "come along, but stay hidden unless I need you."

"Yes," Jade blurted out, pulling her clenched fist into her side. "Where are we going?"

Prudance sighed. "To the Pewterclaw cemetery."

"Why in all the realms would ya be wanting to go to a place like that in the middle of the night?" Toby asked, puffing on the end of his pipe.

"To meet Zoe," Prudance answered. "You should put that thing away, too. The smell will give up your location in a whiff. It also stinks." She waved a hand in front of her face.

"Nobody appreciates a good tobacco anymore," Toby stated. "It has a bad rap, ya know. Them companies add chemicals that make people sick. In the raw, it can be quite medicinal."

"Sure it can," Jade said, pulling the pipe from his mouth. It flew through the air and landed in a garbage bin waiting for pick up the next day.

"Hey," Toby complained. "What did ya do that fer? A fella needs to have a little enjoyment in life. I never saw you throwing out the vampire's green bottle of blood."

Jade's eyes dulled at the mere mention of Gavin. She missed him, even if he did drink blood. How long did it take a broken heart to mend?

"The best way to forget one lad," Toby said, reading her thoughts, "is to find another. It's good advice for the taking. There are others waiting for you to notice. Think about it, lass. Love doesn't have to be restricted to once in a lifetime."

Chapter Thirteen

A cemetery was usually the last place a person plagued by nightmares wanted to go, yet there she was shivering in the moonlight. A howl in the distance made her question if a wolf or shifter was to blame; both were equally as dangerous. Meeting a were-anything at midnight in a place of the dead wasn't going to go well for a witch. Jade, for all intents and purposes, had been labelled one of those.

Since her father's recent election victory, she'd learned a lot about the residents of the magical cities. One particular rivalry saw a clash between numerous shifter clans and prominent witches' covens. It stemmed back a few hundred years and was over power. She was quickly learning that these skirmishes always were. Power and money were the root of all evil. There was little solace to be found knowing Prudance would likely be the first target if it came down to a fight.

The wind howled a warning, a sharp blast slapping her across the face for tagging along. Even the weather didn't approve of her actions. A series of goosebumps formed over her arms. Her thoughts drifted to the two avian guardians that had taken up residence as pictures there. Did they feel the same chills she did?

Their silence as of late frightened her. This was past being an inability to communicate. There was something wrong between the three of them. Lasel and Shelby should have heard her thoughts and at least offered some advice. Even now, as she questioned their relationship, their voices remained lost to her.

A crinkle of leaves under her foot meant fall was around the corner, even though it was far too early for the season. They had Atlantis to thank for that. Weather patterns hadn't completely returned to normal yet. Of course there was a chance Morynx had a role to play in the climate too. No one knew exactly how far the god's abilities ranged.

Her first view of their destination came into focus. The black cemetery gates loomed over top of them. She glanced up at the two stone pillars planted firmly on either side of the iron bars - a gargoyle perched on top each glared down at her. Their eyes followed her every movement.

"They aren't real," Prudance said, reading her mind. "They were put there to ward off evil spies. It was a popular trend in the early eighteen hundreds."

"Are you sure?" Jade whispered.

"Real gargoyles wouldn't be stone at this time of night," Prudance advised. "They'd be off finding trouble somewhere...or causing it." She stopped at the locked gate. Opening her hand, palm up, she caressed a tattoo directly in the centre. A purple glow appeared, making way for an emerging wand. Her fingers wrapped around the shaft. With a quick flick of her wrist the chain and padlock fell to the ground. The gates squeaked open.

"That was easy," Jade said, following her inside. "So where do you go?"

Darkness enveloped them. There were no official city lights within the cemetery itself. A few scattered solar lights cast shadows over gravestones, but none were strong enough to illuminate more than a few inches in any direction. Still, they pressed on, a vibe of desolation accompanying every step. Here, even colours had been frightened into hiding. All that remained were shades of grey against the black of night.

Most of the name markers showed signs of having weathered through ages. Prudance allowed her fingers to glide across each one they passed; feeling the last strings clinging to the life that once flourished crumbling away.

"Stay here," Prudance ordered. She pointed towards a fountain of the dead.

Water flowed from the eyes of skulls piled into a triangular mountain, before collecting in a shallow stone basin below. The clear liquid then recycled creating a neverending circle - the artist's depiction of life and death. Benches circled the unusual monument. Jade took a seat, watching her companion continue on alone.

Prudance didn't have far to go. Only a few gravestones away, sat the woman she had beckoned to meet her - poised as if on display. The scene unfolded before her as an old-fashioned black and white photograph, touched up to add one bright colour for accent: red.

Zoe's dress stood out in the night, bright flames flickering around the bottom hem. She sat nonchalantly, waiting. One foot kicked the gravestone that had become her personal seat. A red high-heeled shoe teetered, threatening to fall from her foot.

"You're here," Zoe called out. "I can feel you. Come out, come out, wherever you are."

"I'm right here," Prudance replied, stepping forward. "I didn't come to play games."

"Why did you want to meet me?" Zoe asked. "Still mad about the salad?" She howled a laugh sinister enough to silence all other noises.

Prudance returned her own chuckle. "No... I want to know what you've done with Joseph."

"Joseph?" Zoe echoed. She wagged one finger in the air. "He always was a ladies man, but I am impressed one short meeting at the bar..."

"Don't be ridiculous," Prudance demanded. "I've known Joseph for years..."

"And he never mentioned you," Zoe interrupted. "I guess you weren't all that important..."

"I could say the same to you," Prudance retorted, squaring her stance to the woman in red. "He never once mentioned any sibling other than Lance. What does that mean?"

"Insolent fool," Zoe bellowed. "Joseph is having a bit of a nap. He was kind enough to allow me the use of his power in the meantime."

"What have you done to him?" Prudance cried, raising her wand. She froze, feeling the icy grip of the dead locking onto her arm.

"Tsk tsk," Zoe said, waggling her finger. "It isn't nice to play with the dead." She howled another equally disturbing laugh.

"Zoe!" Simon yelled.

"Brother," Zoe answered, without looking. "I'm relieved you are well! You have perfect timing... you can join Joseph."

"I'll not be your puppet, sister," Simon replied. "Prudance, you need to take Jade and run."

Zoe cackled. "Then what?" she asked. "Are you going to take me on? You must know you don't have a chance. You never had the power of your brothers. If anything you were... the weakest link." She grasped her sides, the pain flaring up in full force. Another surge left her on her knees, a drop of blood falling from her nostril.

Simon lunged forward, but a single flick of her wrist sent him hurtling back towards the girls.

"Good to see you again, Simon," Prudance offered, still running. "Maybe together, we could best her? I'm not sure we can outmaneuver magic. "

"We need to run," Simon replied. "Next time you two head off on some foolish escapade, at least do some research on what you're getting into."

"Research on what?" Jade shrieked.

"Death magic!" Simon exclaimed, pulling them both by their arms behind him. "Any gravestone is a line to the deceased. Zoe, with all the extra power she has, can easily tap into the land of the dead and call forth anyone."

"I don't understand," Jade said.

"I do," Prudance admitted, her porcelain skin fading a shade whiter. "She planned on calling my ancestors to take me on. Zoe never planned on fighting me herself. She could have wiped my family's existence out in one swoop."

"You're saying any spirit can be called through any grave?" Jade asked.

"If you know what you are doing, yes." Simon glanced over his shoulder. "We need to move faster."

Three heartbeats raged as feet pounded the ground. With the gates in sight, their pace quickened to a sprint. The finish line promised the safety they craved. If they made it to the street, no spirit could follow.

In a land ruled entirely by the dead, not even a master of necromancy had a chance if he chose to side against them. Simon vaulted over a series of gravestones, allowing his two companions the luxury of a straighter course.

The last few steps were critical. He lunged forward, one arm around each girl's waist. Adrenaline fuelled his strength, allowing him to lift the two in one final jump. The three tumbled to the pavement, watching the iron gates close behind them. The padlock and chain flew back into position, sealing danger within the cemetery grounds.

Jade glanced up, catching her breath. Her elbow nudged Prudance. "If they weren't real, where did they go?" she asked, pointing to the missing statues.

Chapter Fourteen

Losing the meddling nosy bodies in the cemetery was an oversight on her part. Zoe simply hadn't anticipated her brother joining that bunch of good-doers.

A pain twinged in her midsection. This time, the burning sensation of bile travelled all the way up her throat. It reached far enough to leave a sour taste on the tip of her tongue, before retreating back to the pit from whence it came. This new affliction was becoming troublesome. It prevented her from enjoying the rewards she was reaping.

Her two brothers were exactly where they needed to stay: behind her. She needed to focus on the task at hand. She had her wedding to plan and a new throne to claim. The word goddess rolled off her tongue and lips perfectly formed until a lingering putrid taste pulled her back to reality.

A mouthful of chocolate was exactly what she needed to wash away any remaining unwanted flavours. One by one, tiny bonbons popped between her lips until not a single piece more could fit. Still chewing, she pulled the mesh netting aside, glancing down at the group of workers carrying her to the mysterious cavern's location.

"Are we almost there yet?" she complained. "I'm quite bored with travelling."

The team of men supporting her compartment exchanged glances.

"Almost," Majesta replied, quickening her pace to have a peek inside. "We should be there anytime according to these maps. Maybe five minutes tops."

Zoe removed a tan safari hat to use as a fan. "This heat is horrid." A piece of ice from under her precious chocolates slid down the front of her shirt, offering her momentary relief.

Majesta nodded towards her employer. "Fanning probably isn't a good idea. It feels refreshing, but it actually increases body temperature from the movement. You'll end up hotter in the long run."

"Thanks for the advice," Zoe scoffed. "I have no intentions of fanning myself for long. One of the workers can take over once we arrive."

Majesta pulled at her own shirt sticking to her skin. There was no relief from the humidity coming. In these parts the overnight lows still held temperatures well above what the rest of the realm was used to.

Even her short blonde hair proved to be fairing no better than her clothing, clinging to the sides of her face and drenched in salty droplets.

For most women, sweat was an appearance killer that led to disasters in the form of running makeup and frizzing dos. The young ancient artifacts specialist was an exception to that rule. On her, perspiration beaded like fine condensation on a cold glass, leaving a glossy shine behind that gave her complexion a healthy glow. The smile permanently etched on her face displayed to the world her love of hard work.

"You do realize we need these men to do manual labour on the site when we arrive," Majesta explained. "There won't be much time for them to serve you."

"You do realize," Zoe replied, "I am in charge and they will do what I ask." She returned her attention to the red nail polish drying on her nails. Her lips puckered, blowing gently over the newly-applied coating.

"Of course," Majesta agreed. "It's entirely up to you how long it takes. We could be here for a day or two... or it could take months. You decide how the worker's time is best spent." Her pace quickened, moving to the front of the expedition.

"Fine," Zoe muttered. Her teeth came down in the centre of her fingernail, snapping it in half. "I'll get the vampires to keep me cool. I still owe them for escaping my witches tour." Holding her hand out in front of her chest, a grin formed on her lips. The missing nail grew back within a minute, perfectly rounded and ready for a coat of shimmering red.

Her body jolted forward, then back. The nail polish bottle crashed on the ground, its contents spilling out at her feet. "Watch it!" She sighed, pulling out her wand to finish the job. Being put on the ground only meant one thing: they had arrived. It was time to greet the natives.

"Who are you?" Gavin asked, emerging from a tent of his own. "What are you doing here?"

"Gavin, isn't it?" Zoe asked, stepping out of her enclosure. "Kasper Deogole sent us at Malarchy's request. We are here to examine the find." She held out one hand.

Gavin glanced at her hand, choosing to ignore the offering. "And what, exactly, do you plan to do?"

"Plan to do?!" Zoe shrieked. "We plan to do whatever we choose to do..."

"We are here to look at the symbols," Majesta interrupted. "I'm a specialist in the field and I'm hoping I can decipher some meanings. I've seen the pictures. This is an exciting find. I'd like to get started as soon as possible."

"If you've seen the photos we took, you must know the cavern isn't stable," Gavin explained. "Another tremor could be extremely dangerous."

Majesta nodded. "Yes," she replied. "Trust me, I know the risks. We've brought a team to assist in stabilizing the area as much as possible. I don't need to tell you, this could be a significant find."

"Alright," Gavin said, crossing his arms over his chest. "What's the first move?"

"I'll be going in to assess what we are looking at and the danger potential," Majesta explained. "Once I confirm it's safe enough to proceed, the rest of the team will set up the magics we need to keep the ceiling intact. At that point, I can begin tests and translations."

"Are you sure going in alone is a good idea?" Gavin asked. "Perhaps an escort might be appropriate."

Majesta's eyes brightened, her features softening. "I appreciate the offer, but this is my job. I understand the risks. The fewer people involved, the better. A single misstep and everything could slip through our fingers. I don't want to risk losing everything."

"Besides," Zoe added, "she won't be alone. I'll be joining her."

Chapter Fifteen

Malarchy shook his head, assessing the bruises and cuts of the three youths standing before him.

"I won't even ask," he said. "It'll only upset me. We have enough to worry about walking in on Kasper this early in the morning. Or did you forget the plan?"

"Zoe is hiding my brother somewhere," Simon blurted out. "She's syphoning off his power for her own use. I need to find and free him."

Malarchy rubbed his face. "Fine. I'll handle Kasper with Esmerelda. The rest of you can search for Simon's brother." He paused. "How dangerous is your sister?"

"Very," Simon replied. "She was an extremely competent witch to begin with. With Joseph's abilities added to her own, she is going to be hard to stop."

"Do we know if she is inside?" Stan questioned. "Any chance we might get lucky and she took the day off?" He scratched his head, his finger breaking into two pieces. He collected the bits and placed them under his hat. "Oops. I'll fix that later. Nothing a little bonding glue can't handle."

"I'm assuming we don't know Zoe's whereabouts," Malarchy said, shaking his head. "Let's try not to aggravate the situation any more than we have to. We don't need a magical battle between the Department of Secrecy and our own. There's enough on our plate as it is."

"Agreed," Stan stated, scratching his nose with one of his still-intact fingers. A little too much pressure and the side of his nostril crumbled, leaving a hole straight through to the inside cavity. "Oops. I can fix that later." He entered the building first, taking stock of the lobby. His head popped back out the door. "All clear."

Malarchy pushed passed him with a huff. It was going to be a long day. With a grip on Esmerelda's arm, he disappeared around a corridor leading to Kasper's office.

"Hello again," Petra said, hustling over to greet the remaining visitors. "Is this a raid?" She giggled.

"Yes, ma'am, it is," Stan answered, taking off his hat to bow. Finger parts scattered on the floor. "Sorry." He chased down each bit, returning them to their hiding place.

"We know," Simon said, holding up one hand. "You can fix it later." He turned his attention back to the aid. "Is Zoe here?"

"No," Petra answered. "She left on a secret expedition this morning. I have no clue where to, either. It's all very hush-hush. Kasper might know the details."

"Has there been any sign of her brother?" Prudance inquired.

"None," Petra admitted, her attention fixed on the constable. She gasped, mortified.

Stan glanced at her, perplexed. He looked up, realizing his hand was resting on the breast of a statue of a woman. He jumped. The sculpture he had been leaning on toppled over, crashing to the ground.

"Sorry!" he called out. "I can fix it!"

"Can you tell us where her office is?" Prudance asked. "We need to take a look inside."

"I can't be a part of that," Petra answered. "I could lose my job. I won't be the one to tell you Zoe's office is across from the director's. Will you be taking the constable with you?"

Simon fired off a wink, ignoring her final question. "Thanks. We'll catch up to Malarchy and be out of your hair in no time." The three disappeared around the corner.

Stan finished propping the statue back up, the end result being not quite as straight as the original had been. He picked up the remaining broken limb. After making several attempts at fitting the piece back in place without success, he pulled his jacket around it. His lips puckered, attempting to whistle a tune.

"What are you doing?" Petra asked.

"It ain't easy to whistle after death," Stan answered. "I used to be quite good at it."

"I meant with that arm," Petra complained. "You do know that was an expensive artifact."

"I do now," Stan said. "Don't worry. I can fix it." He glanced around, realizing he was the only one from the raid left in the lobby. "Do you know where they went?"

"Oi!" Petra shook her head, walking away.

Chapter Sixteen

Simon exchanged glances with Prudance. One of them needed to turn the handle. Neither moved. The cold silver metal reflected their apprehension, toying with their self-esteems. Who knew what traps awaited anyone who dared to enter Zoe's domain.

"Out of the way!" Toby exclaimed. "We'll be here a fortnight before either of you find the nerve." He pointed at the wall, magics flowing from his finger. A second entrance appeared, this one open.

"I thought you only used magic when someone made a wish," Simon said, side-eyeing the leprechaun on Jade's shoulder. "I didn't hear anyone ask."

"It be true," Toby answered. "I don't normally offer my aide outside of business. However, it should be noted that we leprechauns are also not known for our patience. In this case, it seemed a good idea to intervene. What I don't understand is why we are still standing here.

I found the way in. You two can manage to go through, can't you?" He winked playfully. "Unless you're scared, that is."

Jade snickered. She hadn't admitted it to anyone, but Toby was growing on her. The truth was, if loneliness had been one of the sins, she would have been guilty and an easy target. Having someone around was a comfort she wanted to indulge in.

"We got this," Prudance said, holding up one hand. One foot inched closer, testing the stability of the ground before crossing the threshold. The last of her purple ensemble disappeared. "Nobody's home."

A smirk formed on Simon's face, eyebrows waggling. "Guess it's safe," he joked, heading through.

"Lass," Toby said, "don't be taking this the wrong way, but yer friends are a bit on the odd side."

Jade laughed, entering the office last. "This is big," she said, taking stock of the room. "Twice the size of my father's even."

"That's my sister," Simon muttered, picking up a diamond paperweight shaped after an engagement ring. He chuckled. "What girl could say no to this?"

"Do you think it's real?" Jade asked.

"I'll take a look," Toby offered, appearing on the desk the ring had been found on.

Simon returned it to its original spot, watching the leprechaun go to work. A monocle appeared in his left hand. Holding it to one eye, he leaned down, his nose almost touching the surface of the rock.

"It is most definitely real," he announced. "I don't think I've seen a finer piece of ice in quite some time. Whoever bought this paid a pretty penny for it."

"It goes with her swollen head," Prudance scoffed. "I wonder who the lucky gent is."

"I think we can assume it's Kasper," Simon replied. "That's the only explanation for how he's been treating Esmerelda. The question is, how?"

"What do you mean?" Prudance snickered. "Women have been bewitching men throughout all history."

"While agree with you on that," Simon started, "I'm not sure Kasper qualifies as a normal man. He would have defenses in place to avoid such a thing. The director isn't the sort who would be happy being made a fool of."

"Point taken," Prudance agreed, rummaging through the over-sized desk. "There's nothing in here except office supplies. What do you think she actually does?"

"As little as possible, I would imagine," Simon scoffed. "This would be an ideal set-up for her. I didn't expect her to go to the lengths that have been suggested, though. She might be a psychopath, but family used to mean something to her."

"What do you think is in there?" Jade asked, pointing. "It looks out of place."

The others exchanged glances. "I think this is a case of not being able to see the forest for the trees... a red door in a green room and we are searching through a desk." Simon laughed. "There must be something hidden in there."

"Why would you think that?" Toby asked, rolling his eyes. "Just because only one of the four of us noticed it?"

"It's a type of illusion magic I haven't seen before," Jade announced. "No one was meant to notice it."

"Then why paint it red?" Prudance snickered. "That seems a bit counterproductive."

"More like egotistical," Simon suggested. "Zoe must be fairly confident that her magics weren't going to be noticed. The red is a symbol of her own satisfaction. I am impressed you saw it."

"It wasn't completely clear," Jade explained. "At first it was an odd feeling... when you look at something and on the surface it seems ordinary, but you still know something isn't quite right; a displacement of sorts. The thing I don't understand is when I realized it was there, it became clear."

"As it did for us when you pointed it out," Simon added, rubbing his chin. "It's almost as if a part of her wanted it to be found."

"I guess we should find out what clues little sis left us." Prudance chuckled. Her jovial expression disappeared as the closet door swung open. "Joseph!" she shrieked, running to his side.

"Don't touch him," Simon ordered. "We don't want you being caught in whatever spell Zoe put on my brother. Step back."

"We have to help him!" Prudance cried out.

"While I agree with you on at least one thing," Simon replied, "it isn't as easy as it would seem. We need to figure out the safest way to free him. Zoe is no amateur magician. She's as witchy as they come. If she truly can utilize my brother's abilities as well, she could be as deadly as any foe we've met before."

"I am not without my own abilities," Prudance scoffed. "Need I remind you of my heritage?"

"Be that as it may," Simon said, circling the chair his brother was frozen in, "it takes far less skill and power to put a spell on than it does to take one off. Unless we know something about what happened here, all the magics in the world won't break Joseph free."

"So what do you suggest?" Prudance questioned. She folded her arms over her chest, her eyes following Simon's every move.

"If I may," Jade squeaked, not wanting to become a part of the heated conversation. Her face flushed red as cold stares darted towards her.

"Yes," Prudance said, tapping her foot.

"His wand," Jade continued, her voice cracking. "His wand is stiff."

"That's what she said," Toby blurted out. He slapped one knee, breaking out into hysterics. "You have to admit, that was perfect timing."

Using her thumb and finger, Jade flicked the leprechaun off her shoulder. He landed on the empty display case. "This is no time for immature jokes," she warned, wagging a finger in Toby's direction. "I'm serious."

"I see what you mean," Prudance said. "It looks as if he was picking up his wand."

"I read the files a while ago," Jade muttered. "I'm sure the reports indicated Kasper had stripped both Joseph and Zoe of their wands."

"You knew my family was alive?" Simon questioned, raising an eyebrow. "Why didn't you tell me?"

"You didn't ask," Jade explained. "Honestly, I didn't think of it until now. I may have a bit of a mental separation when it comes to your brother." She sucked in a breath of air. "He did kill my mother."

"Forgot about that," Simon replied, averting his gaze from hers. "I can see how that might affect a person."

"Wait," Prudance said, shaking her head. "Joseph was the one who killed your mother?"

"You seem surprised," Simon stated. "You did say you knew Joseph, didn't you?"

"Yes," Prudance whispered, staring at the ground. "I suppose he was amazing as a friend, but deadly as a foe. I knew about his life and what he did, but never thought the fallout would hit quite so close to home. You must hate him."

Jade forced a smile. "I do," she admitted. "But I also feel sorry for him. I've learnt a lot in the time I've been in this realm. Most of it can be attributed to the fact that sometimes good people do terrible things because they believe it is right. I'm not saying I want to have Joseph over for dinner, but he deserves a chance at redemption in life as much as anyone else."

"You are a wise lass," Toby stated. "Few could forgive a man for murder."

"I didn't say I forgave him," Jade replied. "I said he deserves a chance to redeem himself... not to me... to himself. There is a difference. I will never forgive him for my family's loss."

"Do you think he can hear all this?" Toby asked. "I'd hate for him not to know where he stands when he is free."

"I think you can bet on it," Simon replied, pointing to a single tear cascading down his brother's cheek.

Prudance stopped short of trying to wipe it away. "So if the wand is where the spell originated, how does that help us?"

"We use our own magic to remove it from the equation," Jade suggested. "Once he is no longer in contact with it, theoretically he should return to normal."

"Alright," Simon said. "Here goes nothing." He aimed wand at wand, summoning all of his power. His brother's merely wobbled.

"Don't let up," Prudance said, adding a blast of her own magics into the struggle. The wand wiggled trying to free itself from its owner's tight grip, but remain in place.

Jade watched the conflict. She glanced at her own wand, wondering what good her abilities would be if her companions together weren't strong enough. Mustering every ounce of courage she had, she aimed the green gem tip, altering its course slightly from the others.

"What are you up to?" Toby whispered.

A flash of green magic attached itself to Joseph's fingers, prying them apart. The wand wobbled, inching slowly from his grasp.

"It's coming out!" Prudance screamed.

A blast sent all four flying backwards. The wand jutted upwards, exploding upon contact with the ceiling. Sparks showered down, igniting flames. Smoke wafted up from the embers. The shrill sound of the fire alarm was followed by a dowsing of water.

"That took you long enough," Joseph sputtered. "I would have thought the two of you could have solved that a bit faster... and with less mess." He glanced at the mixture of wet soot covering all of them.

"No need to be grateful," Prudance huffed, crossing her arms over her chest. She turned her back to him.

A wicked smile crossed Joseph's face. In one swift motion, he grabbed Prudance and pulled her into his arms. There was nothing gentle about the kiss that followed. He was starved for her lips, and had no problem letting it show.

"I've missed you," he whispered, playfully nipping her earlobe.

"Why didn't you tell me you were okay?" Her eyes searched for the answer in his before the words finished forming.

"I lost everything," he replied. "I didn't want you to see me like that... a bartender in a one-star tavern. I was afraid of what you'd think of me. I was afraid you wouldn't want me anymore."

"Is that really what you think of me?" Prudance questioned, tears threatening to fall.

"You have to admit, we were both a piece of work back then," Joseph said. "You were every bit as nasty as I could be. I'm not sure understanding was a part of our vocabulary."

Prudance chuckled, hiding a sniffle in her sleeve. "I suppose we were," she admitted. "My pride..."

"My ruthlessness," Joseph said. He turned to face Jade. "For what it's worth, I am sorry. My father..."

"I know," Jade interrupted. "I know your story. I have no interest in your apologies."

"If it's just the same," Joseph said, "one day I hope to be able to make amends with your family."

"I'm not sure any of us are ready for that," Jade admitted. "But you can help us finish what we came to do."

"And what might that be?" Joseph asked.

"Free Kasper," Jade replied. "Hopefully it isn't too late. Let's go."

"Wait! You'll need this." Joseph pulled a syringe from his pocket.

"I haven't seen one of those in a long time," Jade said, eyeing the needle. "Are you saying Kasper is under the effects of your father's memory-altering potion? I thought all of it was destroyed."

"At least one vial made it out," Joseph admitted. "Zoe implanted a new life for herself in Kasper's mind. Lance gave me these before we parted. They were a worst-case scenario solution."

"Great," Jade mumbled.

"Isn't this a good thing?" Prudance asked. "We can give Kasper the shot and he'll be back to his old horrid self."

"Yeah," Jade replied, frowning. "Except if his behaviour is linked to the potion, then he isn't a part of our other little problem."

"If it isn't Kasper," Simon said, "it's probably Zoe that is infected."

"We won't know that until we find her," Prudance stated. "I think we best get this antidote to the director and figure out where Zoe went."

"Maybe one of you could fill me in on the other problem along the way?" Joseph asked.

Simon threw his arm around his brother's shoulders. "You have some catching up to do," he said, leading the way out of the office.

Chapter Seventeen

"Not that I'm not fond of seeing you, Malarchy, but what the devil are you doing back here so soon?" Kasper asked, a scowl etched on his face. "I could use a few less visits in general. If you are here about the possible god leak, I've sent a team to evaluate and contain."

"I appreciate it," Malarchy replied, moving aside. "I'm actually here with a mutual friend." He motioned for Esmerelda to enter and have a seat.

The colour faded from Kasper's face, leaving a blank expression along with it. He tapped his temple with two fingers.

"Kasper," Esmerelda whispered.

The director nodded, his gaze avoiding his visitors'. "I... I... I," he stuttered, followed by a hoarse clearing of his throat. The tapping quickened. "I have a lot of work to do. Is there a reason why you've come?"

"I was worried about you," Esmerelda stated. "It's been a while and you haven't returned any of my calls."

"Is that the whole purpose of this visit?" Kasper questioned.

"I was concerned you might be hurt," Esmerelda suggested. "Has anything happened?"

"No," Kasper replied, his bottom lip jutting out as he shook his head.

"Nothing at all?" Esmerelda pried. "Are you sure? Maybe a sore spot?"

Kasper sighed. "Malarchy, what is really going on here? There is nothing wrong with me, but I am seriously starting to wonder about the two of you."

"Dad," Jade said, peeking her head in the door.

"Please come in," Kasper stated, tossing his pen in the air. "I had no idea you brought the whole family. Anyone else?"

"Director," Joseph said, accepting the invitation. "It's been a rather long day."

"What in the realms happened to the lot of you?" Kasper asked. "You look like you've all been run over by a street cleaner."

"Perhaps a garbage collection truck would have been more appropriate," Malarchy snarled. His icy cold gaze held contempt for the oldest of Cornelius' children. "I'd be happy to take out the trash."

Jade linked her arm with her fathers. She caressed his hand, shaking her head. For a moment, she wondered if the sin they were facing might actually be Wrath. Her father had every right to be enraged; Joseph killed his wife. There was nothing that could change that.

"Long story," Joseph replied, rubbing the chills out of the back of his neck. "To make it a bit shorter, you may want to use this." He tossed the syringe on the director's desk. It rolled, coming to a stop as it met a pen.

"The antidote to the memory-altering potion?" Malarchy asked, arching his eyebrows. Curiosity provided momentary relief to the other emotions flowing through his veins.

"Apparently, Zoe had a vial stashed," Jade explained. "When the director showed up at the tavern she worked at, she seized the opportunity. Kasper has been under her control this whole time."

"So Mornyx had nothing to do with this?" Malarchy questioned.

"That we don't know," Simon answered. "There's a good chance Zoe was the target of the puppet master - gluttony being the loyal servant of the week."

"And I suppose Joseph had nothing to do with any of this," Malarchy scoffed.

"How could he?" Jade asked. "He was locked in a closet. Zoe was syphoning his power to boost her own."

"Will someone please explain to me what is going on?!" Kasper bellowed.

"Just take the antidote," everyone else in the room ordered in unison.

Kasper rolled up a sleeve and plunged the syringe in. "Happy?!" He slouched backwards, catching his breath. "What just happened?" His eyes darted back and forth.

"Esmerelda can fill you in," Malarchy offered. "I think your team might be in danger. A trip south might be in order. You should rest a day or two."

"My team?" Kasper asked. "What are you going on about? I don't recall sending a team anywhere."

"Look at the calendar, Kasper," Esmerelda suggested. "You probably don't remember anything that recently happened. I'm assuming you don't remember standing me up."

"Good god," Kasper groaned. "Is that the date?"

"That is the date," Malarchy replied. "We leave you in capable hands."

"Oh," Joseph said. "I'll be needing my real wand. The one Zoe tricked me with was a fake. It is only fair. I did give you the antidote."

Kasper glanced from face to face before turning behind him to unlock a filing cabinet. He reached inside, his hand retrieving a long wooden puzzle box. A sinister grin shadowed over his face as it lobbed through the air.

"There you go," Kasper said. "Figure out the answer to the puzzle and the wand is yours."

"That's hardly playing fair," Joseph replied, examining the possible combinations. "There were no strings attached to what I gave you."

"Perhaps," Kasper said leaning back. "But Malarchy has the antidote in his possession too. You merely sped up the process of my recovery. I'm also not entirely convinced you had nothing to do with what happened."

"Fair enough," Joseph said, using the puzzle to salute the director. "I'm sure I can figure this out."

Kasper laughed. "Only one person in my history has been able to decipher one of my contraptions and that was my mother. Good luck."

"Ah," Stan said. "I found you. Is everything alright?" He glanced through the sea of glares directed towards him.

"I see Pewterclaw's finest are working overtime again," Kasper joked. "I'm not sure trading in Safron for this one was an upgrade."

Esmerelda snorted a laugh in her usual nasal tone. "It's good to have you back," she said.

"I believe I have quite a bit to make up to you, my dear," Kasper replied. "Perhaps we could start with dinner."

"What did he mean, I'm not an upgrade?" Stan asked. "Safron was a murderer and a crook."

"Let's go, Stan," Simon said, patting the officer on the back.

The force caused an eyeball from its socket. It hit the floor, rolling down the corridor with the constable in hot pursuit.

"I can fix that!" Stan yelled, disappearing from sight.

"About that dinner... you might want to try cooking yourself," Joseph suggested. "Zoe was a little hard on your expense accounts. Going out might not be in the budget for the next few centuries." The door closed before another word could be said.

Chapter Eighteen

"Set up a perimeter," Majesta called out to her crew. "Nobody comes in until I clear the area." She glanced at Zoe. "Are you sure you want to take a chance?"

"Pffft," Zoe answered. "I can handle a few loose rocks. Let's go." She pulled out her wand, using the tip for a light source. "Might as well leave the flashlights. It's in the reports they are nothing more than dead weight inside there."

Majesta tossed her lighting equipment to the side and followed. "We should stick to the outline. We don't know how many unexplored tunnels might be down here."

"That's what I'm doing," Zoe snapped. "Do you think any of this is true? Could there be a god locked away inside these walls?"

Majesta's smile widened. "I've been going over what I could see of the markings in the pictures and I believe it could be true. There are a number of legends that refer to fate of a god of darkness. This fits the descriptions perfectly."

"A real live god." Zoe cackled.

"I'm not sure if anything will be alive," Majesta suggested, "but what we do find sealed in here could be of enormous value. I'm guessing there are treasures and power hidden away."

"Is that it?" Zoe asked, pointing her wand towards an orange glow.

"It is," Majesta confirmed, moving ahead. She ran her fingers over the crack. "It's bigger than in the pictures."

"Can we blast it open?" Zoe asked.

Majesta pushed her companion's wand away. "No," she said, her voice stern. The ever-present smile faded for the first time. "No magic will open that barrier."

"Then how do we see inside?" Zoe asked, her hands placed firmly on her hips.

Majesta glanced around. A pink tongue appeared, wetting her small lips. "Up there," she said. "The dial. It's moved as well. My guess is when the hands move it forces the barrier open a bit more."

"It looks like a clock," Zoe said, straining to see above them, "except for the one part that is spinning quickly. What does that do?"

"I have no idea," Majesta admitted. "It must control where the other hand stops, somehow. If we can break that code, we might find a way in." She crouched down to unpack her tools.

A crooked smile crossed Zoe's face. What need did she have for tools and science? She had everything necessary in her grasp: magic. With the addition of Joseph's strength, there was nothing she couldn't achieve. Her wand pointed upwards. A shower of sparks hailed down around them as magics collided.

The pain in her midsection returned, sending her to her knees. Her wand remained steady, a stream of power drilling through a golden barrier.

"Stop!" Majesta yelled. "You'll bring down the whole cavern." She grabbed Zoe's arm and dragged her to a wall.

A puff of orange smoke drifted up from Zoe's skin. Her breath laboured. She collapsed, her energy spent.

"Stay there," Majesta ordered, moving a few inches to examine the extent of the damage.

The ground rumbled as the dial creaked forward another notch. A shower of dirt and pebbles rained down on them, before a larger quake widened the crack. Larger pieces of the ceiling fell, crashing to the ground. A cloud of dust overtook their senses.

"Run!" Majesta screamed. The word was lost in the boom of the cave collapsing.

Chapter Nineteen

"To what do we owe the honour of more politicians?" Gavin scowled. "Wasn't Kasper's team enough for you to make sure we were behaving?"

Jade moved beside her father, linking arms. "One of the team Kasper sent we believe is being controlled... a woman named Zoe."

"That piece of work," Gavin scoffed. "She's inside the cavern with an ancient artifacts and symbols interpreter."

Jade's grasp tightened on her father's arm, her legs wobbling. "What's happening?! Is that thunder?"

At first, they all remained planted steadfast, processing the situation. The sound had all the qualities of a battle between the clouds, but it wasn't coming from above. The vibrations were under their feet.

"Is someone using dynamite?!" Malarchy stiffened his arm, bracing his daughter's weight.

"No... not dynamite. It's another tremor," Russ replied, his voice barely audible over the sound of falling rocks. "The dial must be moving again."

"Zoe's in there!" Simon yelled. He took one step forward before the trembling ground forced him to his knees; a payment for his insolence.

"We have to wait it out," Gavin ordered. "We won't do anyone any good if we end up needing to be rescued ourselves."

"How long does this usually last?" Joseph asked.

"This is the longest one yet," Gavin admitted. "I think something angered the mountain."

"Or the god within it," Toby suggested.

"I see the leprechaun is still here," Gavin snapped. "Does he do anything other than sneak peeks down your shirt?"

Jade grabbed her collar, pulling it closed. "You don't!" she exclaimed.

"Hardly ever," Toby replied.

Malarchy snatched the little man off his daughter's shoulder by the seat of his pants. After depositing the leprechaun into his side jacket pocket, he turned his attention towards the dust escaping from the entrance to the cave.

"We don't need any distractions at the moment," he said. "This is now a rescue operation."

The mountain roared one final time, rocks and dirt spewing out of its mouth. Silence followed.

"Is it over?" Jade asked, releasing her hold on her father. She let both arms stretch out to her sides, taking one step forward.

"It is," Gavin said, walking by her in his usual stride. "Anyone brave enough to go inside?"

Jade bit her top lip, her arms falling to her sides. There was no sense offering, the others weren't about to let her step foot anywhere near the mountain; although she wondered about Gavin. He didn't seem to care at all what happened to her. How had things gone from heating up to ice cold between them?

"I'm going," Simon said, his wand ready. "Zoe may be a lot of things, but in the end she is still my sister."

Joseph put his arm around his brother's shoulders. "I'm in all the way too."

"If you two are going to see the light of day again, you'll need my help," Prudance stated. "I just found you..."

"And I owe it to Kasper to find out what happened to his team," Malarchy said. "Here's the plan. We secure inch by inch, having the stabilizing team follow in our footsteps. They can make sure the area is secure for the way back."

"I'll get them ready," Gavin offered, his pace turning to a light jog.

"Jade..." Malarchy started, turning to his daughter.

"I know," Jade answered. "I have to stay here."

"It's too dangerous for you to be anywhere near what's happening," Prudance said. "If the dial did move again, we have no idea how long it will be before whatever god is imprisoned in there can escape."

Jade folded her arms over her chest. A sigh escaped slightly parted lips. From where she stood, it was only a few minutes before her friends and family disappeared completely from her view. Their fates rested in the heart of the mountain now.

"They'll be fine," Toby said, appearing back on her shoulder.

She flicked him off. "I better not ever catch you looking down my shirt."

Toby tucked his head into his knees mid-flight. His landing involved a series of rotations, rather than a face plant. Coming to a stop, he stood, wobbling.

"It takes more than a few whiskeys to make me this lightheaded," he chuckled. "As for my behaviour, I apologize. I may have made an unconscious glance or two when we first met, but that be the nature of a man. You are an attractive woman."

Jade felt the heat rising in her face. A red flush surfaced, deepening with each passing moment. "That's no excuse."

"It isn't," Toby agreed. "But it be the truth. Now that I know you, I wouldn't think of doing such a thing. You have me word."

"Why should I trust you?" Jade asked.

"Honestly," Toby answered, pulling on his beard. "You shouldn't."

"I shouldn't?" Jade echoed.

"Aye," Toby said. "I'm not a good person. I've done some terrible things in my life."

"How is this helping your case?" Jade asked.

"Because," Toby explained, "you have bewitched me. I am bound to my duties, but I am also bound to you. I would not put you in harm's way if I could help it, lass. That... I promise you."

Jade felt the familiar rush of heat overtaking her face. Her lips parted, but no words formed.

"A new boyfriend?" Gavin asked, shaking his head.

Jade watched her vampire walking away. Her mind screamed for her body to chase after him, but her legs refused to obey.

Chapter Twenty

Simon lifted his wand above his head, stabilizing the rocks above. His brother inched by with Prudance using her magic on the next section. Kasper's men scurried about behind them, setting metal poles with mirrors in place before balancing their magics between the rods to form a force field barrier.

"As long as those are in place, the area will remain secure," Malarchy explained.

The procession continued for several hours, Prudance and the two princes taking all the risks with the back-up team using them to their advantage.

"Over here," Simon called. "I can see a woman's legs. She's partially covered."

Malarchy rushed forward, kneeling beside the body. "It's the ancient symbols expert. She's alive," he called out.

Majesta moaned as Malarchy removed fallen debris from her body. A layer of ground-in dirt covered her clothing, her short blonde hair greyed by dust.

"Can you hear me?" Malarchy asked.

Majesta coughed, using his extended arm to pull herself into a sitting position. Her eyes fixed on the ceiling, mouth open but revealing nothing.

"My sister," Simon blurted out. "She was in here with you. Do you know where she is?"

Majesta glanced past him at a pile of fallen rocks. Tears pooled in her eyes. "She was there," she mumbled. "It all happened so fast."

Simon rushed to the spot, prepared to fire magic at the rubble. His brother pulled him back.

"It's too dangerous," Joseph said. "If we move any of those rocks, whatever is behind them could tumble on top of us. I haven't unlocked my wand yet."

"Our sister could be under there," Simon argued.

"If Zoe is under those rocks," Joseph began. He bit his lip, pausing for a moment before continuing, "she won't be coming out."

"What if she's alive on the other side?!" Simon cried out. "What if this is nothing more than a wall?"

"If that were true, brother," Joseph answered, "she'd find a way out herself. She has her wand."

"She could be hurt," Simon complained. "We can't leave her to her own devices."

"I'm afraid there is no choice," Majesta interrupted. "I can confirm that the integrity of this whole cavern is at stake if we move any of those rocks." The first aid kit in her hands popped open. Teeth grinding, she poured some antiseptic over top of the worst of her cuts.

"Perhaps it would be best to dress your wounds outside," Malarchy suggested, watching the woman unravel some gauze and apply it to a gash on her arm.

"No can do," Majesta replied, forcing a smile. "The team will have this area stabilized enough for me to stay."

"You can't be serious," Prudance blurted out. "You need medical attention."

"What I need," Majesta argued, "is to decipher the meaning of all of this." She motioned to the spinning device on the ceiling and the widened crack. "In case you missed it, the dial moved. I need to figure out what we are up against before it does it again."

"It's dangerous," Malarchy stated.

"I knew it would be before I came," Majesta answered. "This is what I do. I'll be fine. Ask the men to bring in my supplies and another excavation kit. I seem to have lost mine. I'll send a full report as soon as I have data."

"Is there anything else we can do?" Malarchy asked.

"Leave it to me," Majesta answered. "I'm the expert. In the off chance I might need an extra set of hands, ask your vamprite crew to check in once in a while."

Malarchy chuckled. "I'm not entirely sure they will listen," he replied. "But I will ask. Keep in touch."

"I will," Majesta said. "I'll let you know if there is any news of your sister as well. I do hope she is safe somewhere. We can't lose faith."

"Thank you," Simon muttered, turning to head out of the cave. He stopped just outside the entrance, allowing the rays of the sun to warm his face. He pinched between his eyes.

"Is everything okay?" Gavin asked.

Joseph patted his brother's back. "Dust in the eyes," he replied. "It'll get you every time."

"The team?" Gavin questioned with an arched brow.

"Majesta is fine," Joseph replied, loosening his collar. "Now that her team has put up a safety net, she wants to stay inside to begin her evaluations."

"And..."

"Our sister is missing," Simon blurted out.

"We'd appreciate it if you could keep an eye out for her," Joseph added. "She is not without talent. We keep hope in our hearts."

Gavin nodded. "Understood."

The two brothers began to walk away. Simon stopped, glancing back at the vampire.

"Fix things with Jade," he suggested. "She doesn't deserve what you are putting her through."

"And I suppose if I don't, you'll be happy to take care of her?" Gavin questioned, squaring his stance to the brothers.

"Me?" Simon asked, the beginnings of a smile forming in the corners of his mouth. "Not me. That doesn't mean you don't have competition, though."

"The leprechaun," Gavin mumbled, shaking his head. "There isn't much I can do about that at the moment."

"Why not?" Simon asked.

"It's complicated," Gavin replied. "Maybe someone else is what's best for Jade. I need to consider that as an option. Whatever is inside that mountain, it's about to change all our lives."

"Only if we let it," Simon replied, heading off to rendezvous with the rest of the team.

"He has a point," Joseph said. He fired off a quick salute before catching up to his brother.

Chapter Twenty-One

"According to these notes," Jade said, leaning back in a comfortable chair in her father's office, "we can confirm that the latest puppet was in fact gluttony. That's three down and four left. I don't think we are faring well."

"We aren't any closer than we were before," Prudance commented. "We seem to be one step behind no matter what we do."

Jessica placed one hand on Prudance's shoulder. "Don't worry. We'll find a way to save your mother and stop this whole mess from happening."

"How?" Jade asked, her eyes glossed over.

"What do you mean?" Jessica questioned. "We'll figure it out. We always do."

"No... we don't," Jade muttered, her bottom lip quivering. "We haven't figured anything out. We don't know any more than we did when I began having the dreams."

Malarchy sighed. "I know it's frustrating," he said. "But we have to have faith."

"Faith in what?" Jade questioned. "In a god? In Mornyx? In Raward? We don't even know if either of them actually exist."

"We know something does," Simon interrupted. "Whether it's a god or a super buff vampire doesn't matter. What does matter is we keep going. What does matter is that those who lost their lives because of this are avenged."

Jade nodded. How could she not agree? To her, Zoe was a faceless name on a list. To Simon, she was family. Her mind wandered to her own brother. He didn't hold what she had done in their homeworld against her. She smiled... sibling love was unconditional.

"There is one thing I think we may be overlooking," Krissy squeaked from the corner.

"Please don't keep us waiting," Malarchy said.

"Zoe didn't have any ties to Jade," Krissy said. "At least none I can see. She didn't come in direct contact with any of us either."

Malarchy blinked twice. "That would suggest..."

"Jade might not be the intended target after all," Krissy said. "Perhaps the dreams are meant as a more general warning." She stepped out of the shadow of a bookcase.

"Why me, then?" Jade questioned, slouching back further. "Why not Dan in accounting?"

"Do we have a Dan in accounting?" Malarchy asked, a smile crossing his lips as the words escaped.

"You know what I mean," Jade complained.

"I don't know," Krissy admitted. "I'm only saying the pieces aren't fitting together right. We are missing something. I think we should consider alternate possible targets to be on the safe side."

"And who would they be?" Jade asked.

"Maybe one of the vamprite or Majesta," Jessica suggested. "They are in the thick of things."

"I disagree," Prudance argued. "When I was being controlled, I was targeting Jade. I hated her. If pride hadn't been my master, wrath was waiting next in line."

Malarchy rubbed his chin. "I think we should all take a step back tonight. Try to have a good night's rest. Tomorrow we can contemplate alternate possibilities."

Jade's mouth opened, but never had a chance to say a word.

"That's not an idea," her father said. "It's an order. We are of no use to anyone tired. Tomorrow we can start fresh."

Jade glanced at each of her companions, conceding to the agreement in their eyes. There would be no help from her usual friend. She glanced at the black birds pictured on her arm.

I wish you'd talk to me, she thought. *I could use your advice about now.*

The girl speaks to us, Shelby squawked. *I suppose you feel we are at your beck and call.*

She has asked for our help, Lasel replied to his mate. *It takes two to make a relationship work.*

I am far too tired to be bothered trying to make anything work. Shelby complained. *You help her if you want. I'm going to take a nap.*

I'm sorry, Jade. Lasel said. *She hasn't been herself lately. How can I help?*

I'm not sure you can, Jade admitted. *I'd feel better if you talked to Shelby, though. I'd like to make amends.*

I can try, Lasel responded. *Until then, is there anything you need to discuss?*

No, Jade lied. *It can wait. I think Willow was right. There are some things a person needs to figure out on their own.*

Is this one of those times? Lasel questioned.

Yes, Jade replied. *I believe it is.*

What will you do?

Jade laughed. *The same thing every girl does...I'm going to take my dad's advice. A good night's sleep might just be what I need. Tomorrow brings with it new light and hope.*

Good luck, Miss Jade, Lasel said. *May tomorrow hold all the answers you seek.*

Author's Message

I hope you enjoyed reading Gluttony as much as I did writing it. Be sure to watch social media or my website for more *Surviving The Sins* novellas coming soon.

Thank you for choosing my story! If you enjoyed this book, please browse through some on my other titles currently available.

ABOUT THE AUTHOR

C.A. King is the recipient of several awards, including: The Hamilton Spectator Readers' Choice Award for 2017 Best Author; The Brant News Readers' Choice Award for 2017 Best Author; Readers' Favorite award in the short story/novella category; the 2017 SIBA Award for Best New Adult; the 2017 SIBA Award for Best Novella; 2018 Readers' Favorite International Book Awards: Gold Medal in the Fiction - Supernatural genre; and 2018 Readers' Favorite International Book Awards: Bronze Medal in the Fiction - New Adult genre

Currently residing in Brantford, Ontario Canada, she lives with her two sons. She began her writing career after the tragic loss of her parents and husband. Redirecting her emotions through writing became therapeutic in her battle with depression and in 2014 she decided to publish some of her works.

Other Titles from C.A. King

The Portal Prophecies

These great titles in C.A. King's The Portal Prophecies series are available now at most online book retailers:

A Keeper's Destiny

A Halloween's Curse

Frost Bitten

Sleeping Sands

Deadly Perceptions

Finding Balance

Volume I (Books 1-3)

Volume II (Books 4-6)

The prophecies are the key to their survival. Can they solve them in time?

Shattering the Effects of Time

Join the Shinning brothers, Jessie, Dezi and Pete as they set out on a quest to save their younger sister. No magic known to them or their friends has ever been able to reverse the grip of time. A few legends, however, exist mentioning ancient items that may hold the key to do exactly that.

This brand new series will take you on a search for the Fountain of Youth and Mermaids; a quest for the Holy Grail; a trip to visit Daryl the mountain guru, in the hunt for the Cinamani Stone; on a search for Ambrosia, the food of the Gods; and other adventures.

Surviving the Sins: Answering the Call

The prophecies are being rewritten. This time someone is using the seven deadly sins: Lust; Gluttony; Greed; Sloth; Wrath; Envy; and Pride, to unlock an ancient evil. The book falls into Jade's hands to answer destiny's call. Can she survive the sins?

Surviving the Sins: Pride

No one is safe when a witch's pride is at stake.

Prudance is back in Pewterclaw, and she isn't about to give up her prestigious status without a fight - especially not because of vampires. As an eighth-generation witch, she plans to do whatever it takes to stop the proposed new legislation from becoming law, including waking the dead for help.

Humility isn't in her vocabulary. With an ego spinning out of control and ancestral power at her fingertips, Prudance weaves a plot to keep Jade and Gavin separated. Will it be enough to satisfy the spirits she summoned?

When her pride costs more than she bargained for, someone has to pay the tab - but who will it be?

Surviving the Sins: Lust

What Mother doesn't know won't hurt her.

Lucinda has spent her entire existence running The Organization and looking after Mother's needs without complaint. That's about to change. A burning desire had manifested inside her - one she could no longer deny... Lust.

When Constable Safron Black shows up unexpected with news of an imprisoned God, Lucinda unravels. With power fuelling her passion, she'll do anything to make Morynx her mate.

****

Jade and her friends find themselves at a standstill. They have already failed to stop Pride from completing its task and they haven't located any victims for the other six sins. A strange fire in the municipal office puts them hot on the trail of what could be answers. Will they be in time to stop the dial from moving and further opening the way for Morynx?

When Leaves Fall: A Different Point of View Story

Ralph wakes up to what others only experience in a nightmare. Chained to a shed, he has no idea where he is, or who his captor is. His memories a blurred at best. As the days press on he finds himself experiencing a roller coaster of feelings. Hunger, thirst and pain become his only companions. Flashbacks of a happier time are all he has to keep him going. As his situation deteriorates, he finds himself doubting the very things he wants most - a family.

When Leaves Fall is a dramatic-thriller with a twist. Keep the tissue box close for the ending.

Tomoiya's Story

A Vampire Tale. She had a secret but she wasn't the only one who had something to hide.

Book I ~ Escape to Darkness

Book II ~ Collecting Tears

Book III~ Coming Soon

Peach Coloured Daisies: A Cursed by the Gods Story

He couldn't die. An ancient curse meant she always did. This time, that was going to change - one way or another.

When Daisy's grandmother, her last living relative, passes away, she doesn't know where to turn. Things go from bad to worse when a local psychic tells her about a curse. Alone and confused, she ends up in front of her college professor's office, ready to cry her heart out in his arms.

Matt Demi might be the son of a God, but he's living the life of a cursed man. He's had to watch the woman he loves die on her twenty-first birthday countless times. Nothing he does seems to be able to affect the outcome. When she shows up at his office scared out of her wits by a psychic's prediction, he vows this time will be different.

With only three days, Matt will need to embrace a side of him he swore off long ago to save her, but will he lose himself in the process?

Flower Shields: A Four Horsemen Novel

Meet the four horsemen: Michael, Gabrielle, Uriel and Raphael. For centuries their job has been to guard the gates of hell, making sure they never open. Without the keys, there was never any real threat. That's about to change. There are rumours on the horizon that demon followers unearthed scrolls that explain exactly how to find the lost keys. This new battle is a race to see which side locates them first.

Michael couldn't care less about the love story behind how and why the world was created. In fact, nothing matters to him other than keeping the gates to hell closed. If one of the lost keys ever fell into the wrong hands, all humanity would be doomed. He's not going to let that happen - at any cost.

****

Tara's life is nothing short of a disaster. She's managed to flunk out of college with about the same amount of dignity as every relationship she's been in. The only constant in her life has been her love for flowers. When she's attacked at work, a stranger comes to her aid. Michael might be good-looking, but he's also arrogant, bossy and crazy. He's also her only chance to figure out who attacked her and why. Should she follow her heart and trust him - or listen to her head and run?

Drawing Strength From Words: A Four Horsemen Novel

Meet the four horsemen: Michael, Gabrielle, Uriel and Raphael.

For centuries their sole purpose has been guarding the sealed gates to hell. Without keys, there was never any real threat. That was about to change...

For Gabrielle, protecting mankind was merely a job for which she received little credit. The vast insecurities of men altered history itself, portraying her as a masculine brute. Taking a back seat to her brothers seemed the right thing to do, but left a bitter taste in her mouth and an impenetrable barricade shielding her heart.

****

Ryder bounced around the system from the moment both his parents were killed. Between that and run-ins with the law for crimes he never committed, it seemed the whole world was conspiring against him. Never growing attached to anyone was rule number one: a rule he'd never broken until a white-haired vixen, with blocks of ice on her shoulders, walked right into his life. Melting through those frosty layers became all that mattered, even if that meant sacrificing himself in the process.

Miracles Not Included

A heartfelt romantic story about: life; love; loss; and learning to love again. If only life came with instructions and a warning label ~ Miracles Not Included.

****

Chris was born to be a writer. Even the smallest of details couldn't pass without notice, often becoming part of a plot for her next novel. The one thing she never saw coming was her husband's sudden illness.

Jason loved his wife from the moment they met. Nothing could ever change that - nothing except the death sentence he'd been handed - a terminal cancer diagnosis.

His story was ending: Hers was starting a new chapter and more than one miracle was needed to turn the page.

Twisted Tales of a Dead End Street

A paranormal mystery laced with comedic undertones: Twisted Tales of a Dead End Street.

Nine neighbours were invited to the mysterious dinner party at 9 Nine Street. Their host, the owner of the mansion, had more planned for the evening than just roast beef.

When the secret of their quiet street was revealed, everything changed, blurring the lines between the tangible and the paranormal.

Was the number nine the difference between life and death? Would any of them survive long enough to uncover the truth? They would each soon find out this wasn't a simple case of who-done-it so much as one of what was being done and by whom.

Shot Through The Heart: A Faerie Tale

A tale of two worlds - one filled with magic; the other void of it. But what happened to those trapped between the two? Adelia was about to find out...

Magic and structure were the foundations of her existence. Temptation controlled the ability to destroy everything she knew. The world of men held a powerful allure over her heart, waking that which had long been dormant. It enticed her, snagging her in a web of emotions.

A decision had to be made. Was feeling love for the first time worth sacrificing magic and immortality?

Do Not Open Until Halloween

When eighteen year old Caitlin agreed to babysit her eccentric Aunt's two cats and house, she had no idea that Justin was finally going to ask her for a date the same weekend. Torn between family and crush, she chose to take her best friends' suggestion to heart, arranging a small Friday night gathering. Little did she know a fairy was about to crash the party with trouble hot on her wings.

Caitlin will have to dig deep to find even a smidgen of belief in magic or there won't be any hope of saving her new friend from being hunted.

In this young adult fantasy, award-winning author, C.A. King, explores the answer to one of the questions readers have always wanted to ask...

Where do fairies come from?

www.ingramcontent.com/pod-product-compliance
Lightning Source LLC
Chambersburg PA
CBHW052145170626
46812CB00004B/1598